PIG IN THE MIDDLE

Sam Llewellyn was born in the Isles of Scilly and brought up on the north coast of Norfolk, on whose outlying sandbars he got to know many seals. He now lives with his wife Karen and two sons, Willie and Martin, in the Welsh Marches – except when they are at sea in their ketch, *Loon*, or watching seals, dolphins and stags on the remote west coast of Scotland, which is the setting for *Pig in the Middle*.

A keen and experienced sailor, Sam Llewellyn has written several adult thrillers set in the world of sailing, as well as *Pegleg*, a seafaring adventure for young people.

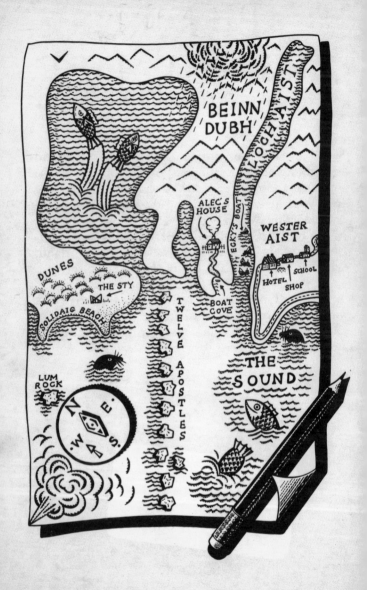

PIG IN THE MIDDLE

SAM LLEWELLYN

Illustrated by
MICHAEL TREVITHICK

WALKER BOOKS
LONDON

To Will and Martin

First published 1989 by Walker Books Ltd
87 Vauxhall Walk, London SE11 5HJ

This edition published 1990

Text © 1989 Sam Llewellyn
Illustrations © 1989 Michael Trevithick

Printed in Great Britain by Cox and Wyman Ltd, Reading
Typeset in Hong Kong by Graphicraft Typesetters Ltd

British Library Cataloguing in Publication Data
Llewellyn, Sam
Pig in the middle.
I. Title
823'.914 [F]   PZ7
ISBN 0-7445-1420-7

Chapter One

"No, no, no, *no*," said Miss Dummer.

The strangled notes of the Fingal's Cave overture died in the pale green corners of the schoolroom. Oh, blimey O'Reilly, thought Alec Whean, lowering his recorder from his lips. Here she goes again.

"It's so *romantic*," said Miss Dummer, flapping her plump white hands at the end of the pale pink arms of her jersey. "Are we *feeling* it? Let me *explain*!" And she was off.

Alec gazed out of the window and let it all gurgle over him like liquid mud. Miss Dummer spoke of fairies, elves, highland chieftains and bards. She was very keen on that sort of thing.

Beyond the classroom window, a short slope of tufty grass ran down to the weedy shore of Loch Aist. Down the loch, which was not a lake but a ten-mile arm of the sea, a streak of spring sun had scraped past the west flank of Beinn Dubh and lay over the water. The electric clock on the wall said there were three minutes of school to go. Alec very badly wanted to be out there.

"So can you feel it, Alec?" said Miss Dummer. She sounded as if she had potatoes in her mouth. "Kate?"

Kate Robertson, one of the trio, gazed at Dummer out of her green eyes, stuck out her jaw and nodded. Alec knew she thought the same of Miss Dummer as he did.

The final third of the trio said, "I thought Alec played *lovely*." Alec's insides shrivelled like a prune as Doris MacNab gazed at him through her long dark eyelashes and simpered prettily.

"If he spent more time on the recorder and less on the bagpipes, he might make a real *musician*," said Miss Dummer, tucking her top chin into the two below it. "Now then. Again."

The recorder trio took a deep breath and raised its instruments to its lips. Doris was still looking at Alec, who was staring back at her with the glassy expression of someone who is doing one thing and thinking about another.

Miss Dummer raised her podgy hands. "And a-one, two, three —"

Blast off, thought Alec. He moved his foot over to the switch on the wall and flicked it with his toe. There was a sudden whirring and a sound like an air-raid siren chasing a herd of cows round a car park.

Miss Dummer's mouth became round. Her hands clutched her hair.

Alec caught Kate's eye. Kate was purple, shoulders shaking. Doris MacNab had turned pale and was clutching the piano for support. The noise was ear-splitting.

Miss Dummer leaped to her feet and wrenched open the door of the broom cupboard. Alec knew what she was seeing: the nozzle of the school Hoover taped to the mouthpiece of a set of bagpipes. He felt very proud. It was an impressive noise, much better than the recorder trio.

Miss Dummer's foot stamped on the Off switch of the vacuum cleaner. "Alec!" she cried. "I'm confiscating those bagpipes!"

"GAAAAH!" screamed someone in the next room.

"Oh jings!" squealed Kate Robertson. "Yon's Heavy Murdo!"

Miss Dummer expelled her breath. "I'll deal with you later," she hissed, and strode across the room, her weight making the plank floor shudder. Heavy Murdo was an expert at hurting people and like many experts he enjoyed his work. "MURDO!" she cried, stumping next door, where a crowd of children, woken from their quiet reading by the sound of the pipes, had gathered round a collection of struggles and yells in the far corner.

Alec's moment of triumph gave way to boredom. He was fed up with old Dummer, with the fug in the room, with the stupid Fingal's Cave overture, with Doris MacNab and her white socks and her soppy stares. He had had enough.

Miss Dummer's voice sounded like a circular saw in the other room. Soon it would return and start up again for his benefit. The clock said it was past bell time. Alec eyed the window, then looked across at Kate. "I'm away," he said.

Kate nodded. Alec knew she could be relied on to put up a strong rearguard action. Doris gasped and raised a hand to her rosebud mouth. "Ah'm telling!" she cried.

Kate turned on her. "One sound out of you and I'll biff you up to Pluto," she said.

Alec climbed on to the windowsill and unlatched the catch. He dropped lightly to the ground and ran across the tussocky grass, towards the first grey outcrop of granite that would mask him from the school.

The air smelt of salt and wet grass from the morning shower. When he was round the rock he paused, panting, and looked back.

Wester Aist Primary was a low, grey building with a bell-tower on one end, standing on the narrow white road that wound southward along the loch shore, past the anchorage with its fishing boats and on round the coast. To the west of the school was Morag's shop and the Hawtrey Hotel, where the men of Aist drank and Englishmen stayed for the fishing. To the east were the meadows through which the river wound and a couple of fields of potatoes, tilted on the lower slopes of the mountains. Above the fields, the grass and bracken began, rising to a knife-edged ridge, black against the hard blue of the sky, where the peregrines nested.

All this Alec saw, but did not look at. He knew it off by heart, because he had lived across the loch for eleven years, and had been coming to Aist Primary for six. What he was looking for was the splodge of pink against the school's grey stone which would mean that Dummer was giving chase.

It did not come. And mingled with the shriek of gulls above the loch was a new sound, a sound like the distant preaching of the Twelve Apostles to seaward when a big sea rumbled in their crannies.

Alec knew the sound. It was the sound of a dirty great riot in the classroom.

He turned and ran. As he ran, dodging the tarry old humps of timber and wrecked fragments of trawl net, he felt a moment's regret for his bagpipes. But Dummer would give them back in a couple of weeks. It had been worth getting them confiscated to see her face. Besides, he still had his chanter.

He did not slow down even when he was well out of sight of the school. There was a boat at the lochside: Ecky Bruce.

"Gie's a lift, Ecky," he said. Ecky rowed him across. He jumped out and trotted up a steep track through the heather. He came this way every day and it did not occur to him that it was steep. High and to the right, his parents' house perched in a tangle of sheds on the shoulders of Beinn Dubh: grey stone, one storey, a window either side of its front door. The sight of it depressed him. He ducked behind a rank of gorse bushes, breasted the ridge and started down the other side at a long lope.

Below him was a tiny horseshoe of water, flanked by beaches of grey rock. In the exact centre of the horseshoe was a small boat with a stub mast. The bay was so small that the boat seemed to fill it. Alec felt the memories of school and the gloom of home slithering off him and began to be cheerful.

The average person might not have spotted much to be cheerful about in Alec's life. His father painted pictures and fished for salmon returning to spawn in the River Aist. At least, he had once. He had stopped fishing before Alec could remember, in order to concentrate on playing the fiddle and drinking whisky. There were supposed to have been reasons for his giving up work; but Alec didn't know them and his father never discussed them.

His mother did all the work of the croft herself: she needed a lot of help. Alec helped her, but the strain of it all put her in a bad mood most of the time. And sometimes, like now, Alec just liked to be by himself, not filling swill-buckets or mucking out the cow, or most of all getting yelled at by his mother for things he had not done.

He slid down the last three feet of weedy rock, pulled the boat ashore, climbed in and rowed out of the little cove and into the loch. There was no wind; the water was flat and black, reflecting the shadowed slopes of the mountains that rose on either side. Alec rowed west, keeping under the shore, out of sight of his house and the school. He wanted solitude, and he knew where to find it.

Chapter Two

Wester Aist is seven-eighths of the way down the south shore of Loch Aist. Alec pulled the last mile to the open sea with no trouble, seen by nobody except the men in the wheelhouse of *Driller Killer*, Ivan McPhee's fishing boat, heading in from pulling nets in the Sound. Ivan was Heavy Murdo's dad, a huge and evil-tempered man known as Ivan the Horrible. *Driller Killer* worked up to her mooring buoy off the village and Ivan and his four crew rowed ashore and stumped into the bar of the Hawtrey Hotel.

The houses vanished behind the Point and Alec rowed into the flat waters of the Sound.

Suddenly, there was no sign that he was not the only person alive on earth. Above him the gulls cried. To seaward, the tide roared in the Twelve Apostles and sloshed through the flat rocks where the seals slept like huge grey sausages. But of human beings, there was no trace.

He headed north for a mile, until the mountains moved back and the foreshore became less steep, and the heather of the slopes gave way to trees. Then he pulled towards the land. A bay opened out, a huge rolling beach of silver sand, backed by dunes on which grew thickets of dark green pines. Solidaig. The bow of the dinghy hit with a soft *crunch*. He picked up the anchor and jumped out over the bow, disturbing a flock of black and white oystercatchers that rose, piping, and fluttered off.

The sand at Solidaig rolled up to the dunes like silver waves. Except at very low tides, the troughs of the waves were full of water. Some were deeper at one end than the other, so that when the tide went out they remained as lagoons, reflecting the sky. The largest of the lagoons was cut off from all but the highest spring tides by a long blade of rock like a dam. It was even big enough to have a name: the Sty.

Having anchored his boat, Alec marched across the wide, white beach to the black blade of the Sty. When he reached it he climbed up and went to his usual place, a cup-shaped hollow in the granite, precisely the right shape for an armchair. The roar of the sea was dull in his ear, backed by the hiss of the huge Solidaig silence. Pulling a packet of Opal Fruits from his pocket, he settled down to think.

Life was, frankly, pretty unpleasant. Home was bad: but when you have had trouble at home ever since you can remember, you tend not to let it get too much on your nerves. No; the main trouble was the ghastly Fingal's Cave overture, Murdo and Dummer.

Dummer had arrived from England last year. Since then she had told the school about four times a day how much she loved Wester Aist; its river, mountains and sea, and in particular its people.

Also, she said there were fairies at the bottom of her garden and expected the practical children of Wester Aist to see them too. Alec had looked, but all he had been able to see was a rotting Land Rover and some enamel buckets with the bottoms kicked out. Dummer had taken a great shine to Alec. She had decided he was a Bright Boy, who needed Bringing Out of Himself, which was why she had forced him to play the ghastly Fingal's Cave overture on the recorder, an instrument he hated.

16

Finally, and worst of all, while she coached the recorder trio the rest of the school had to do Quiet Reading. If there was one thing Heavy Murdo hated it was people whose recorder playing meant that he had to do Quiet Reading.

Heavy Murdo was big, and wide, and he had fists like lumps of knobbly concrete. Alec pulled up his dark blue jersey and looked at the blackish bruises mottling his ribs. Heavy Murdo never hit you anywhere that showed, but that did not mean he did not hit you.

Alec slid down from the rock and waded into the edge of the Sty. Under the glass-clear water, the sand was carpeted with winkles that grew legs and walked away from the shock waves his feet made. Hermit crabs. Thousands of Miss Dummers, thought Alec; creatures that picked up someone else's shell the way she had picked up Wester Aist Primary.

Sploosh, said something out in the Sty.

Alec looked up quickly. The water was only twenty feet across here. In its centre, a circle of big ripples was expanding. His heart was bumping in his chest. It was as if someone had thrown a stone. But the nearest human being was two miles away by water, ten by land.

There was a new noise to his right, a sort of hiss. He looked round sharply.

Two eyes looked back.

They were round and black, and set in the front of a sleek grey head with long whiskers that sprouted on either side of the nose like an RAF moustache. The head floated in the water fifteen feet away. The body was a pale shadow, hard to see because of the reflections of the sky.

"Hello, seal," said Alec.

It stared back with such intelligent eyes that Alec half expected it to answer.

"What are you doing here?" said Alec.

The seal blinked and sank out of sight. It surfaced after a minute, closer.

Alec knew a lot about seals. Every flat rock had its colony of grey bodies, basking or quarrelling. In the breeding season, the rookeries on the islands beyond the Twelve Apostles were carpeted with mothers and young. That was in the autumn. It was spring now, but this one was only just out of its baby fur.

"You're too young to be on your own," Alec said. Seals did occasionally breed out of season. This one must have come in here on the spring tides a couple of weeks ago. They tended to stay fairly close to their mothers, at this age. Maybe she had forgotten; or maybe...

"Ivan the Horrible carries a rifle on that boat of his," said Alec. "They don't like seals, the fishing guys."

The young seal watched him with its big black eyes. Slowly, it drifted closer.

Time I was off, thought Alec. There were animals to be fed and if Dummer had talked to his mother he would be in enough trouble already, never mind not doing his share of the chores. Then a thought struck him. "Hey," he said. "When did you last eat?"

The seal opened its mouth and shut it again.

"I know," said Alec. "You're hungry." He walked into the shallow water and raked with his fingers. They met round, solid lumps: cockles. Perhaps this seal's mother had not had time to teach it to hunt. He tossed it a cockle.

The seal followed the shell with its head and looked at Alec as if wondering whether or not it should clap.

"Thick creature," said Alec. He locked the hinges of the cockle shells together and twisted sharply. One of the shells came apart. He threw what was inside to the seal. The seal sniffed at it. Then, with a smooth roll of its grey flank, it turned in the water and ate it. After that, it turned back to Alec.

This time there was no doubt about the message of the whiskers and the eyes. It liked cockles and it wanted more.

An hour later, Alec's fingers were sore with

raking and twisting and the seal seemed no fuller. But the sun was setting into the clouds to the west; soon night would be falling, and it was not at all clever to be in the Sound after dark.

As he trudged across the low hills of sand to his boat, he looked back. In the Sty, a black dot sat in the middle of the sheet of grey water reflecting the high cloud and the pinkening sky. It looked lonely, that dot. Alec knew how it felt.

But tonight, he was not lonely. He was going home probably to catch hell for wiring up his bagpipes and slipping out of the school window before the end of the recorder trio practice, and for not being there to help with the animals. But the thought of that black dot waiting in the Sty was strangely comforting.

Chapter Three

As Alec walked up through the little yard in front of the house, the lights of the windows flung yellow squares over the mucky ground. The animals had been put away, he noticed, with a lurch of the heart. From the bothy came the long whine of a fiddle playing a strathspey. Which meant that his mother had tossed his father out of the house, having done the animals herself. It was going to be bad.

It was bad.

Alec's mother was a tall, wide woman with a rawboned face. She had a broad, freckled forehead and a habit of running her fingers through her hair so it stood straight up. The straighter it stood, the worse her temper. Tonight, it was vertical.

"Alec," she said in a low dangerous voice. "How nice of you to come."

"I was feeding this seal," said Alec, recognizing the signs.

"Seal?" said his mother, her tired eyes glittering like green traffic lights. "Seal? Well now, I've been feeding the *pigs*, and the *cattle*, and the *chickens*, and the *geese*." With each word her voice grew louder, and she took a step towards him. He stood still, teeth clenched, knowing what was going to happen. "And the *cat*, and the *dog* —"

On the word *dog* her big red hand came round and gave him a buffet on the ear that made his head ring. "And now I've fed all those animals, I'm no' going to feed you, Alec Whean! And Miss Dummer says you've been playing her up at school, and your father's not pleased." Alec screwed up his face against what was going to come next.

It came.

"He wasted himself," said his mother. Her voice was loud and hard. "Him with two university degrees. And even if he'll sit idly by and watch you go the same way, I won't. Now get to your bed!"

So he went up to his room in the join of the roof and lay and stared miserably at his collection of sea shells until his mother screamed up at him to put the light out. From the yard, the sound of his father's fiddle rose, long and plaintive, playing "Carrickfergus". And Alec worried – not about wasting himself, or about Dummer; but about the seal. The seal had family trouble, too. He and the seal had to stick together.

Tomorrow was Saturday, so there would be no school till Monday. The seal's face rose before his eyes. Was it still there? If it did manage to flop across the sand and went looking for fish to eat in the Sound it would be in trouble. The currents were terrible. It was not unusual to find young seals drowned on the beach...

Hunger woke Alec next morning at five o'clock. Outside his window, the world was grey with dew in the dawn. He made himself a giant sandwich in the kitchen; cheese, ham, a sprinkling of cornflakes (his speciality) and double bread on the outsides. The first one went down without touching the sides, so he ate another, then ran round the chilly yard, feeding the animals. His father was in the bothy, sprawled on the hay, an empty whisky bottle by his side, his left hand still holding the neck of the fiddle. His face looked grey and old, but he was half smiling. Alec threw a blanket over him and laid the fiddle in its case. The only time his father ever looked happy was when he was asleep. Alec was glad that he would be out of the way by the time he woke up and he and his mother started shouting at each other.

The path down to the boat cove was wreathed in mist. The breeze was blowing away the fog from the sea, but strands of it caught in the islands like sheep's wool on a barbed wire fence. Halfway down, the path looped round a crag of granite. A voice behind the crag said, "Alec?"

He jumped nearly out of his skin. A small, thin figure in jeans, a jersey and a down jacket got up from the crack in the rock. "Kate," he said. "You're early."

"I wanted to catch you," she said. "Dummer's after your blood. Because of the pipes and going before the bell." Her small freckled face cracked into a grin. "Ach, it was brilliant, Alec."

They laughed. Alec, much encouraged, said, "To hell with Dummer. I'm going fishing."

"Can I come?"

"If you want." Monday morning seemed a long way away. There was no point in worrying about Dummer till then.

When they got to the cove there was enough wind for the sail. Alec pulled it up and the ripples gurgled round the boat's bow as he pointed it for the distant cream of the waves breaking in the Twelve Apostles. The land and the gulls' cries sank astern until Alec knew they were over the Crickie, a ridge of rock that came up from a great depth, making an underwater eddy in the tide where fish waited for food. "Let's go," he said. They heaved their red rubber lures overboard to dance twenty feet down among the brown weed.

Within an hour the bucket was full of the olive-green, flapping bodies of saithe. The wind was up now, knocking the occasional white horses out of the cold green waves.

"Will I gut the fish?" said Kate.

"Don't bother," said Alec, and shoved the tiller away from him, feeling the surge as the wind flattened the heavily patched tan sail.

"Where are we going?" said Kate, as the boat heeled steeply and the water started to roar astern.

"You'll see," said Alec. He did not want to tempt fate. He was looking forward to seeing the seal, and the distant silver line of Solidaig had brought back the fear that it might not be there.

The tide was halfway in, the waves breaking angrily on the first hummocks of the beach. Alec let out the mainsail. The nose dipped as the stern went up on a wave. Kate said, "Whee!" as they surfed in, slowed as the water calmed between the two banks of a channel and drifted to the shore.

"Bring the bucket," said Alec. He jumped over the side and toiled up the sand slope with the anchor.

She watched him hack the anchor into the sand, excited, as always, by his oddness. Odd or not, he always seemed to know what he was doing. Herself, she had no idea what was going on. But she loved the pressing silence of Solidaig, so she shouldered the bucket of fish and ran after him, feeling the thump of the hard sand under her heels.

From the top of the slope, Alec could see the Sty. His heart sank. Its surface was smooth as glass, except where the breeze frosted it with tiny ripples.

"What's up?" said Kate, catching up.

He shook his head. He could not bring himself to speak. Until now, he had not realized how much he had been looking forward to seeing the seal. And now there was no seal. He trudged on, though, just in case.

A couple of gulls were strutting by a rock at the far end of the Sty, where the water shallowed. When they saw Alec and Kate, they flapped into the air, shrieking. The sand where they had been was churned up with their footprints.

With more than their footprints. The rock suddenly moved, pivoted on a fat stomach, paddled down to the water's edge.

"What's that?" said Kate. She knew perfectly well what it was, but the expression on Alec's face was so remarkable that she felt she had to ask anyway.

"The seal," said Alec. "My seal. Here, I'll take that." And grabbing the heavy bucket from her hand, he began to run.

The seal ate the first fish in one gulp, and the next, and then the one after that. Only after the fifth saithe did it start to slow down. The sixth it chased round the lagoon, shoving it with its nose like a tiny grey water-polo player before flipping it in the air by its tail and catching it neatly in its mouth. Alec and Kate clapped. The seal gave them a look, the fish's tail sticking rakishly out of the side of its mouth. Then it bowed, the bow taking it all the way under the water.

The last two fish it could not eat, though it tried, chomping at them where they lay in the water.

"Isn't he great?" said Kate.

Alec nodded. The seal was on its back now. It looked like a miniature fat man in the bath.

"My dad was saying Ivan's out to kill some seals," Kate said. "He reckons they're taking fish out of his nets."

Alec's head jerked round. "Rubbish," he said.

"I know," said Kate. His eyes were so hot that he was almost frightening to look at.

"But you know what Ivan's like."

Alec had heard his father talk about Ivan. He'd do anything for money, his father had said. And fish were money, and seals ate fish.

"Maybe he's got a point," said Kate, who had a disconcerting habit of reading his thoughts.

"Nah," said Alec. "My dad says they're clever, so some of them learn to take fish out of nets. That's all."

"So what's Ivan making a fuss about?"

"My dad says Ivan's always got to blame things on someone else."

"Murdo's like that."

"Maybe his dad taught him how."

Alec did not want to talk about Murdo, so he threw the seal another fish. It took a bite, then spat out its mouthful.

"Pig," said Kate.

"It might have felt hungry again," said Alec, quick to its defence.

"Still pig," said Kate. "In the Sty, and all."

The seal heaved itself out of the far side of the lagoon with a definite grunt. It fell instantly asleep and snored.

"OK," said Alec. "Pig."

So Pig, from that moment, it was.

They came back that evening, and the following day, Sunday, twice. The weather was clear and fine, with light southerly breezes, so it was no problem getting round to Solidaig.

On Monday morning, Alec went out by himself, before school. This time, Pig was so pleased to see him that he went almost mad with joy, diving and rolling in the clear waters of the Sty, and taking his last fish a mere foot away from Alec's hand.

Alec had made several good resolutions about getting to school in plenty of time to explain about bagpipes and Hoovers. But Pig was anxious to play water polo with fish heads, and somehow Alec stayed and talked to him until quarter to eight. Which meant that by the time the school bell went at nine-fifteen, his sail was still a tan-coloured pocket handkerchief on the flat horizon of the Sound, and he was going to be at least half an hour late.

Chapter Four

Miss Dummer took Assembly at record speed. Normally she liked her pupils to sing a couple of Gaelic tweed-weaving songs before they made their way to their desks. But this morning, she limited them to "Over the Seas to Skye", instructed them to do Quiet Reading and stumped outside.

On the school porch she gazed at the scrap of tan sail and struggled with her anger. From the schoolroom she half heard the growl of Heavy Murdo threatening a little one, and the screams of the little one as Murdo started trying to skin him alive with a blunt pencil. But she paid no attention.

Miss Dummer was a large, pink blonde, with thick straight hair that fell down her back, and pale blue eyes. She had taken over Wester Aist Primary twelve months previously. She was a terrific Scot, as only Scots can be who have read the complete works of Robbie Burns and Robert Louis Stevenson in a semi-detached house in Bromley, Kent. Miss Dummer's grandmother had come from Oban and had often claimed one of *her* grandparents had been a silkie – a man with a human mother and a seal father. So Miss Dummer considered that the West Coast of Scotland was in her blood. And in the manner of people who wish they were something that they aren't, she was greatly disappointed with the actual inhabitants of Wester Aist.

Some, like Ivan the Horrible and his son Heavy Murdo, she regarded as simply Brutal. Others, like Kate Robertson, she thought of as Misguided. One or two, like Doris Mac-Nab, she thought were Sweet, because they were hard-working, attentive and believed in the fairies dancing among the rusty buckets at the bottom of her garden. Alec Whean she thought of as Awkward, if Bright.

Alec Whean was the best musician in the school. He was reasonably good at other subjects and he was everything that Miss Dummer thought a child of Wester Aist ought to be. But he would not *try*. By trying, of course,

Dummer meant that he would not behave the way she thought he ought to.

As she watched him drag the boat up the beach, hack in the anchor and wipe his sandy hands on his jeans, her heart thumped in her pink woollen chest. She had to make a gesture.

"ALEC!" she bellowed. "COME HERE!"

At the sound of her voice, a peregrine falcon jinked on the slopes above the village and made off for the crags of the Four Bens, inland.

"Where have you been?" she said. The boy's trousers were wet, the cuffs of his jersey ragged.

"Sailing," he said. His eyes were grey and private, and they did not look at her.

"Alec," she said. "This is school time."

"I know," he said, dully.

"So why were you sailing?"

"Don't know," he said.

"And what was all that ... ridiculous business on Friday?"

"Don't know," he said, again.

Miss Dummer snorted with rage, and almost yearned for the days when you could clear up this kind of thing with a few good whacks of the tawse. Then she brought herself up short.

"Well, you can stay in after school and write a composition explaining why," she said. She saw his eyes flinch. Ah, she thought: *got you*. And to quell the beginnings of shame that rose in her at bullying this child, she said, "A *long* composition. Now go inside."

So Alec went in, and sat down in his wet trousers, and got his books out. Staying in after school meant not feeding Pig. But that ought to be all right, because he had left a couple of fish where Pig could get at them if he needed to. He was getting clever, old Pig. This morning, he had caught a fish full-toss. It was more like having a friend than a pet.

The boy next to him nudged him with his elbow. Alec jumped. "Ah," Miss Dummer was saying, in her most sarcastic voice, "how kind of you to wake up. Now you have had your nice rest, perhaps you would tell the class the name of one great poet who drew inspiration from the Scottish mountains?"

Alec looked at her pink cardigan and her earnest blue eyes, and said, "Billy Connolly."

There was a roar of laughter that rattled the windows. Heavy Murdo swung round and looked at Alec out of his meaty red face and said, "He's no' a poet."

"Quite right, Murdo," said Dummer, her big cheeks crimson. "Alec, you can stay in at break."

Heavy Murdo screwed his face into a mean grin. The lesson droned on, about Flora Mac-

Donald and Bonnie Prince Charlie and a lot of other stuff Alec seemed to remember from the tourist guides his mother's bed and breakfast visitors left lying about the house in the summer. Alec thought about Pig.

He did not like what Kate had told him about Ivan the Horrible and his gun. Still, he was fairly sure that when the spring tides came back, Pig's mother might come and look for him. That would be in ten days or so. Until that time, what he had to do was keep him fed, and keep him a secret.

Five minutes before the end of break it started to rain and the other kids came in from the playground. Heavy Murdo was with Kate. Kate looked fed up; Murdo was always following her around and telling people she was his girlfriend. Alec looked up, then back at his composition, which he had started already to save himself time after school.

Someone sat down heavily on the bench beside him, making it creak. He knew by the smell of aftershave that it was Heavy Murdo. He chewed the end of his biro without looking round, then went on writing.

"I hear you've got a seal," said Heavy Murdo in his harsh, niggling voice.

This time Alec did look up. Murdo's mouth was pressed into a mean line.

"Aye," said Murdo. "Kate told me. And you know what I told her?" He paused. Alec kept writing, his heart banging hard. "I told her my dad's got a gun."

"Wow," said Alec, hoping the blood heating his face did not show. "And what else did he get for Christmas?"

"My dad catches fish for a living," said Murdo. "My dad says seals is a damned bluidy nuisance. My dad and some of the lads is goin' out for to shoot some this week."

"Oh," said Alec, trying not to sound interested.

"In the boat," said Murdo. "*Driller Killer*." He put his face close and lowered his voice to a vampire croak. "The sea'll be black wi' bodies. Pangggg!" Murdo made his fingers into a rifle. Flecks of spit sprayed over Alec's exercise book. "And then they get a big sharp knife and they skin 'em. So say goodbye to yer sealie, Whean. Maybe he'd sell you the skin."

Alec stopped writing. He stared at the paper in front of him, but he did not see the paper. Instead he saw the clever, funny face of Pig, watching him from the surface of the Sty. Then he looked up at Heavy Murdo, the lardy red cheeks, the thick spitty lips, the little currant eyes under the mop of black hair.

He went mad.

He whacked his fist into Murdo's face. Murdo yelled with pain and surprise, and screeched, "I'll kill ye, ya wee tube!" Or he was going to say *tube*; what actually happened was that Alec's other fist caught him slap in the stomach of his blue jersey and he said *urgh* instead and fell off the bench on to the floor. Alec had no time to think. He had scarcely realized that he was punching up Heavy Murdo, the hardest man in the school. But he realized now, and knew he had to put him out of action for a while. So he jumped in the air and landed on Murdo's stomach with both knees.

All the girls screamed, except Kate. Alec put his head close to Murdo's gasping goldfish face and said in a furious voice, "If your dad goes near my seal, I'll kill him."

Kate's voice said, "Here she comes."

Wester Aist Primary thundered like a drum as everyone returned to their desks. Then there was a silence, broken only by the sound of Heavy Murdo whooping for breath on the floor.

"Get *up*!" said Miss Dummer.

Heavy Murdo rolled on to his hands and knees. "I want tae tell," he said. "It was Alec Whean."

Dummer's eyes were dark and angry. "There's no call to tell tales," she said. Then, turning to Alec, "I shall see you after school, both of you."

Chapter Five

The rest of the day trudged by with leaden boots. At three-thirty, the children clattered out for the bus that wound up the road, twelve miles under the Four Bens, into the mountains. But Alec lived just across the loch and Heavy Murdo half a mile away in a shiny new bungalow surrounded by his mother's pack of Dobermann pinschers and bits of old engine. So Miss Dummer was not too worried about how they were going to get home.

"Sit together," she said. "In front of me." Alec saw that her face had the mottled look it always took on when she was embarrassed or angry.

They both squeezed on to the same bench. Alec could smell fear and aftershave rolling off Murdo in waves.

"Now, then," said Miss Dummer. "What was that all about?"

Alec opened his mouth to speak, then realized he would have to tell her about Pig. So he shut it again.

Murdo saved him the trouble. "He's got a dirty seal, Miss," he said. Murdo was stupid enough to expect all grown-ups to share his father's views on seals.

"A *seal*?" said Miss Dummer. The mottled look disappeared, and her voice became a dove-like coo. "How *lovely*! Where?"

Alec looked down at the desk. Someone had written DUMMER IS A DOPE on the wood. He said nothing.

"But the class would *love* to see it," said Miss Dummer.

"*I* wouldn't," said Heavy Murdo, sullenly. "Dirty things. My dad'll shoot it, any road."

Miss Dummer's face turned dark red. "*Murdo!*" she said. She lifted her plump hands and for a wonderful moment Alec thought she was going to strangle him. Then her hands dropped and she said in a strange, tight voice, "I wouldn't be too sure about *that*, if I were you! Now, then. Murdo, I will not have fighting. Remember that. Now go."

Murdo left, scowling.

"So, Alec," she said, and her voice was light, almost girlish, "you have a seal, have you?"

"Aye," said Alec.

"*Do* tell us where it is. We'd *so* love to meet it."

Alec hesitated. He had a sudden vision of the beach at Solidaig black with children swarming over the whalebacks of sand. Dummer would be plodding along in the rear in her pink cardigan and tartan skirt, face shining earnestly. And Murdo ... well, even if Murdo wasn't there, he'd make someone tell. Then it would be Ivan the Horrible, and his rifle, and his skinning knife.

Alec shuddered.

"No," he said.

"*Well*," said Miss Dummer, her face flushed with disappointment, "I'm on your *side*, you know."

"Aye," said Alec, thinking of the stupid Fingal's Cave overture. He uncapped his pen and opened his composition book. "I'd best start now."

"Quite," said Miss Dummer, her face mottling again. "Quite. I shall be in the office marking." She turned as she reached the door, and looked back. Alec's head was bowed over his book; his pen was moving. She felt a deep sense of failure. It was sad, she thought; one did everything one could to get through to these children, and look what happened. Still, she thought, with a return of confidence. Wait till they found out what she had up *her* sleeve.

It was quiet in the late afternoon. The breeze sighed in the grass and gulls cried, and a couple of flies buzzed high among the rafters. Alec wrote a long, boring story about sheep, lulled by the tiny rumble of his ballpoint as it travelled over the page. After twenty minutes, he heard a tapping at the window.

He looked up. At the window he saw a headful of brown curls, a pair of green eyes and a snub nose. Above the eyes, two eyebrows were wriggling furiously. Kate.

Alec scowled at her and went back to his composition. The tapping came again. He did not look round. Kate had told Murdo about Pig. She had put Pig in danger.

The tapping was a hammering now. She'll break the glass, thought Alec, with a gloomy satisfaction. Then she'll get into trouble.

"What's that?" said Miss Dummer's voice through the closed office door.

He looked up, despite himself. Kate's face was a mask of excitement. Not like the face of someone who wanted to say sorry.

In the office, Miss Dummer scraped her chair and coughed. Carefully, Alec got to his feet and crept across the floor, avoiding the board that creaked. There was a pane gone here and the caretaker had blocked it up with cardboard, which pupils in detention were in the habit of removing in order to talk to their friends outside.

"What is it?" whispered Alec.

"There's a ship come in," said Kate. "A big trawler. Full of funny people."

"What do you mean, funny people?" said Alec.

"Och, weird," said Kate. "Like —"

At that moment, the chair in Miss Dummer's office scraped and the floor shuddered as her weight came on to it. Alec shot back to his desk. Kate just had time to put the cardboard back in the window before Dummer came in. Her face was flushed and she looked excited.

"Alec," she said. "You can go now."

"But I've no' finished yet —"

"Never mind that," she said. Instead of her pink cardigan, she was wearing a tent-sized sweatshirt, bright blue, with a pattern of turquoise waves on it. Over her bosom was a design of a seagull and the word BLUE. It was a pretty nice sweatshirt, Alec thought, but it made Dummer look as odd as an airship in a bathing suit. "Get along with you."

Alec needed no urging. Ten seconds later he was out of the school door. Kate was waiting.

"You told Murdo about Pig," said Alec.

Kate's cheeks turned bright red. "He shut

my hand in a desk and sat on it," she said. "I didn't tell him where, though."

"You shouldn't have told him anything," said Alec. But he looked at Kate's hand, where a black bruise ran behind the knuckles, and he knew he would have told Murdo just about anything, to get him off that desk. "Does it hurt?"

"A bit," said Kate. And Alec knew that there was peace between them.

"Look, though!" said Kate, pointing.

A long, low ship was anchored in the mouth of the loch. Alec had seen a lot of trawlers, but never one painted in those colours. Its hull was blue and turquoise, with a design of breaking waves. On its bow were painted the words *Pole Star*.

"Let's go and have a look."

"Nope," said Alec. "We've got to feed Pig first." In fact, he was extremely interested in the trawler. But after what Murdo had said he was on tenterhooks to see if Pig was still in the Sty and not shot to smithereens by Ivan the Horrible.

He pulled the boat in, held it for Kate as she came down the stony beach, and climbed on board. The breeze was blowing off Beinn Dubh, so they were able to sail down the loch towards the fishing grounds. Their course took them right under the bow of the trawler with the blue and turquoise paint job. There was a seagull painted by the hawse hole where the anchor cable sloped down into the sea. A bearded man on deck waved.

"Old Dummer was wearing a sweatshirt like that," said Alec.

Kate squinted up at the trawler's super-structure. "Weird," she said. An outboard engine snarled astern.

"Look," said Alec. "Ivan the Horrible's not pleased."

The outboard engine belonged to a Zodiac inflatable which was buzzing past Ivan's rusty fishing boat. The inflatable was flying a flag that said BLUE. Ivan was standing on the deck of his boat. His arm was raised and he was making an extremely rude sign with two of his fingers.

"Weird," said Kate again. "Let's go and catch some fish."

They went on, the nose of the dinghy rock-ing as they hit the first of the swell that al-ways ran in the Sound. The swell was big today; the Twelve Apostles were preaching in their hard, rumbling voices, and the base of the flat islands where the seals basked was white with foam.

"Hello," said Alec, after twenty minutes. "What's that Zodiac doing?"

They were almost on top of the Crickie now, and Kate was unhitching the fishing lines.

"Start fishing," said Alec. The Zodiac was a quarter of a mile away, idling along. "I think they're following us."

"Why should they be?" The line jerked violently in Kate's hand. "Got one."

"Carry on fishing," said Alec. It was a good evening for the saithe. Kate filled the bucket in half an hour. But when the bucket was full the Zodiac was still there, hanging two hundred yards astern. There were five figures in it. One of them was large, wearing a blue sweatshirt.

"That's Dummer," said Kate.

Alec nodded grimly. "They're after us." His heart was beating fast. "They're trying to follow us to Pig."

"So what?" said Kate.

Alec felt the anger rise. Pig was his, and his alone... He stopped himself. "I don't want her to find him," he said. "Or her friends. She'd do something ... silly."

Kate nodded. She knew about the silliness of Dummer. "But we've got to feed him," she said. "What are you going to do?"

Alec had been thinking, and he had decided exactly what he was going to do. He grinned to hide the fear that was tightening his grip on the tiller and making his stomach feel sick and hollow. He said, "Go by the Apostles."

Chapter Six

The Twelve Apostles were a line of rocks that ran out from the shore like a row of unevenly-spaced teeth. When the tide was ebbing and flowing, a salty torrent poured between them like water over a drowned man's jaw.

On this particular evening the tide was low, so eight of the twelve were sticking out of the water. Even so, they were hard to see, because of the halo. The halo was the fog of spray that surrounded the Apostles, spray hurled into the air by their constant chewing at the waves. To Alec, looking along the tan sail and over the bow, the rocks were a line of huge black shapes that came and went behind veils of fog. And out of the fog came the hard, crunching roar of heavy water on rock.

Alec sheeted in the sail. The boat heeled, digging in the bulge of her downhill side. The Apostles grew out of the sea.

When Kate felt the cold spray of the halo on her cheek, she knew she could not do this.

"Check your lifejacket," said Alec.

She saw that his jaw was set tight, his eyes narrow slits as he searched the water ahead for the way through. She opened her mouth to shout at him that it didn't matter if Miss Dummer met Pig, or anyway not enough for them to drown trying to stop her. But she knew that it did matter. Dummer would spoil everything somehow. And it would be Kate's fault if Dummer did, because it was she who had told Murdo about the seal.

Her fingers clamped on the wooden seat. The boat was jumping in the uneasy chop of the sea. But she told herself that Alec knew what he was doing. There was nothing to be afraid of.

The roar of the Apostles was so loud she could hardly hear herself think. The sky reeled above the boat's mast as they went up, up on a wave. A whirlpool opened to starboard with a voice like an elephant pulling its foot out of deep mud. Suddenly there was no horizon, and a sweating wall of black rock was whizzing by on either side. And the sail was flapping, but the rock was rushing past as the tide caught the boat and washed her through the gap at the speed of a cantering horse. The tiller bucked and thrashed in Alec's hand; another whirlpool spun by, then another, making a hole in the sea they could have fallen down without touching the sides. Kate found she was breathing in short, horrible gasps. But the noise was fading. "See?" said Alec. His face was flushed and he could feel his knees trying to knock together. "*Easy*. And we've lost Dummer."

Pig seemed very pleased to see them. He surged around in the Sty, making the water boil with his flippers and showing all his teeth in a big grin before he took his fish. When he had demolished the bucketful, Kate picked up a plank of driftwood and threw it for him. He raced after it and retrieved it neatly. Then he stood up in the water, the plank across his mouth like a pirate's knife, grinning. There was a *crunch*. The plank fell in half, bitten through. He spat out splinters.

"We won't teach him tricks," said Alec. "It's not fair."

"OK," said Kate and shrugged her shoulders. Alec was hard to argue with; or if you did, he usually turned out to be right. For a moment they stood watching the splinters floating on the ripples. "Let's go."

Pig floated upright, watching them walk back across the beach. Kate thought he looked lonely. But she thought it might be silly to say so, so she kept her mouth shut.

Actually, Alec was still shaking from their ride through the Apostles. Now that the excitement had faded, he realized it had been a stupid and babyish thing to do, whether or not Dummer was following them.

They pulled down the loch and climbed out of the boat. As they walked up to the village, there was no sign of Dummer. Heavy Murdo was sitting on the beach in front of the Hawtrey Hotel, eating a sherbet dip. He put his fingers together in the form of a pistol barrel and made shooting noises. Alec ignored him.

"I said I'd get some rice for my mother," he said.

"See ya," said Kate, careful not to say anything in front of Murdo. Heavy Murdo followed her with his curranty eyes and sucked at his sherbet. Alec nodded and walked into the shop.

Morag had a round face, white hair and a floral overall. She was a kind woman, fierce when she remembered to be. But today she was frowning, bending over a packet of something with a bespectacled man Alec had not seen before. When she looked up, the smile she gave Alec was hardly there. "I don't rightly know," she was saying.

"There has to be a list of ingredients," said the man with the spectacles.

"I've been selling oatcakes for twenty years," said Morag in a tight, worried voice, "and nobody asked me yet were they organic or no'."

Alec said, "They're great oatcakes."

The man turned, and looked right through him. "Oh," he said. "Really." He had a thin London accent, a scrubby beard and close-set brown eyes behind his little round glasses. He was wearing a Blue People T-shirt. "And contain animal fat, I shouldn't wonder."

"No animal fat," said Morag. "Only a wee bit of dripping."

"Dripping!" cried the man with the beard. "*Ugh!*" He turned and went out of the shop, slamming the door so the cigarette advertisements rattled.

"*Well*," said Morag, her eyes perfectly circular. "*What* a funny wee man. I wonder what could he mean, organic? He's off that boat, the one that looks like it was painted by children. He said he was a Blue Person. What do they want?"

"I don't know," said Alec.

"I don't think much of his manners," said Morag. Then remembering who she was talking to, she snapped, "And what can I do for you?" to cover her lapse.

Alec bought his mother's rice, shouldered

his haversack, and went outside. Kate was over talking to Heavy Murdo. There was pink sherbet smeared on the corner of Murdo's mouth, and his eyes were mean above his suety cheeks.

"How's sealie?" said Murdo, winking at Kate.

Alec ignored him. So, he was pleased to see, did Kate.

"They make grand dog food," said Murdo, and sniggered. "My dad's practising his shooting, this evening. That'll be the lot for your cuddly wee seal."

Alec looked at Murdo, and grinned. The reason he was able to grin was that he was thinking of the way the cuddly seal had picked up the stout bit of driftwood Kate had thrown and crunched it in half with one easy chomp of its teeth. "When your dad's missed, you can come and give it a cuddle," he said, and ran down to the boat before Murdo could clobber him.

He did not get there.

A big man in a blue jersey was sitting under the wall of the hotel, catching the sun on his jowly red face. As Alec ran past, the man stuck out a boot. It was too late for Alec to stop. He went flying, grazing his knee painfully on a rock. He lay there in agony, hearing Murdo's scornful laugh from up by the shop.

"A word in your ear," said Ivan the Horrible, with a slow stretch of his thick lips over his dirty teeth. "From the day after tomorrow I am going to be shooting seals. They steal my fish and they break my nets. These Blue People have come down to stop me, so I'm going to have trouble with them. I want you to know that if there's any extra trouble from you, I will personally wallop you within an inch of your life."

"Huh," said Alec, acting cocky to show Ivan he was not frightened of him. "I hope they do stop you. And they're not your fish."

"I get money for them," said Ivan. "I need money to live. I work to feed my family. And if a seal gets in the way, too bad for the seal."

"There's enough fish for you and the seals," said Alec.

"No," said Ivan. "There's less fish every year, and more seals. So the seals have got to go."

"My dad says —"

Ivan laughed deep in his belly. "His dad says. Nobody pays any mind to your dad." His face came down towards Alec. Alec could smell stale beer and tobacco. "Not even you."

Alec stared at him. He opened his mouth to tell Ivan to shut up. Then he shut it again.

Alec's mother might yell, and his father might drink, but he loved both of them and he was not about to sit still and listen to Ivan the Horrible bad-mouthing them. The trouble

51

was Ivan was right about one thing. If Alec had listened to his father or his mother, he would never have sailed through the Apostles. And now he had let them both down.

"Just stay out of my way," said Ivan, and spat at a tuft of grass.

Alec turned and walked back to his boat feeling very, very sad.

Chapter Seven

Alec rowed across the loch singing the terrible Fingal's Cave overture loudly and as out of tune as he could manage, to keep his spirits up.

When he got home he ran across the yard, belted the house door open with his shoulder and heaved off his rucksack. When he opened the kitchen door the heat billowed out at him, mixed with the steam of boiling potatoes.

"Come in here," said his father's voice.

He knew that voice. His heart sank. He went in.

Both his parents were sitting at the table. Their faces were hard and set; his father had shaved, which was always a bad sign.

"I'm glad to see you alive," said his father.

"Go on," said his mother. Her hair was on end and there were dark circles under her eyes. "Don't beat about the bush. Tell him."

His father frowned. He hated telling anyone anything. He cleared his throat and said, "You went through the Apostles in your boat. You were seen. I've had Kate Robertson's dad over here. He's not pleased. And nor am I. You could have got yourselves drowned."

Alec started to say something. But the worst of it was, he knew his father was right.

"So your mother and I have decided, no more boat."

Alec had been expecting the worst, but in his wildest dreams he had never imagined it was going to be as bad as this. "But, Dad," he said. "I've got a wee seal. I have to feed it."

"A *seal*?"

"At Solidaig. In a pool."

His mother made a noise like a small, frustrated explosion. "If you spent more time feeding the animals here and less time feeding your seal, maybe your father would have more time for his painting."

Alec's feelings of affection evaporated. He nearly said that his father did not seem to be doing much painting these days. Then he caught the look in his eyes; a look of hurt, almost of pleading.

"Aye, well," said his father, pulling a cigarette from his pocket and ducking to light it so he did not have to look at Alec. "No boat. If you behave well for a fortnight, you'll get it back. Till then, you can go to school with Ecky Bruce."

"And now," said his mother in her that's-all-there-is-to-say-about-that voice, "away and feed the animals. They'll be forgetting what you look like."

So Alec trudged miserably round the mucky yard with the buckets pulling his arms out of their sockets. He gave the calf's food to the pig, and the pig's swill to the calf, and slopped the cow's water into his gumboot, and got shouted at by his mother and had to start again. But he hardly noticed, because of the other things on his mind. Partly, he was furious with Dummer, for trying to follow him to Solidaig. Partly, he was furious with himself, for being stupid enough to sail between the Apostles. But mostly, he was worried about Pig.

If Ivan found Pig, he would shoot him. The only solution was for him to stay at Solidaig, in the Sty. But there were no fish in the Sty. So he needed Alec to feed him. But Solidaig was a ten-mile walk away by land.

There was no answer, thought Alec, rattling the buckets miserably at the pink and black snout of the sow. The sow put her head forward for her ear to be scratched. Alec scratched dutifully. But it was hard to get involved with a pig that would be sent to market in three weeks, and be slaughtered. Not like his Pig.

As he came out of the sty, the long Highland dusk was gathering in the folds of the hills to the east. Suddenly the dusk was full of explosions. They came one after another, giant footsteps tramping down the glen, sending the crows scattering from the black pines.

Ivan the Horrible was out with his rifle, practising.

Chapter Eight

Alec slept badly: he kept waking, dreaming that he was being watched by a pair of big black eyes. Hungry eyes. Next morning after he had fed the animals, he went to check his boat. His father had padlocked the mooring chain. And he had to admit that he had deserved it.

So with a heavy sense of guilt he turned his back on the little cove and trudged round the shoulder of the hill to the slip opposite the school, where Ecky Bruce was waiting. As Ecky rowed him across the loch there were five men on the deck of *Driller Killer*, and a couple of rubber boats with outboards bobbing at her waterline. Rubber boats of a kind useful for creeping up on seals. Waiting for tomorrow, and Ivan's cull.

It was a rehearsal morning. There was something skittish about Miss Dummer; she seemed nervous, like a barrage balloon in a gusty wind. Alec's eyes kept straying out of the window to Ivan's fishing boat; he found it impossible to concentrate.

"*Da dee dardle ar dar*: a-two, three, four," cried Miss Dummer, and began to apply her podgy fingers to the keys in huge, rippling arpeggios. "Now then, recorders!"

Kate Robertson filled her lungs. Doris MacNab eyed Alec meltingly from under the lashes of which she was so proud. Alec frowned at the sheet music as if it was about to spit in his eye.

"And, a-*one*!" cried Miss Dummer.

Three recorders spoke as one. Two of them fluted delicately. Alec's emitted a noise like a frightened steam engine. Doris MacNab giggled. Miss Dummer's bosom heaved under her cardigan. "ALEC!" she yelled. "WHAT IS THE MEANING OF THIS?"

Alec gazed out of the window. The rubber boats were still nudging round the waterline of the fishing boat. "I don't know," he said dully.

"Again," said Miss Dummer. "The concert

58

is in two weeks."

The notes on the page ran round like black beetles. Alec licked his lips. "A-two, *three*," cried Miss Dummer over the roar of the piano.

Again the train whistle.

"Tch!" said Doris, with a cute smile.

Miss Dummer leaped to her feet and slammed the piano. "Alec!" she cried. "If you spent more time practising and less time trying to drown yourself and your classmates on the way to Solidaig, you would be a better recorder player!"

"Yes, Miss Dummer," said Alec. It was hard to concentrate on school, when Pig was starving on Soli —

"What?" he said. "How d'you mean, Solidaig?"

An expression of triumph hovered around Dummer's lips. "I have my sources of information," she said.

Alec's eyes flicked across to Kate. She was staring at her music, her face the colour of beetroot.

"And soon," Dummer continued, "that seal will be in *expert hands*. Much better off."

"Whose?" said Alec.

"The Blue People's."

Alec thought of the trawler and the man buying oatcakes. He had not taken to Oatcakes. If the rest of the Blue People were like him, he did not want them to have anything to do with Pig.

"They are here to prevent the killing of the seals."

"They won't get far against Ivan the Horrible."

"They are a respected body of scientists and conservationists. They know what they are doing."

"Oh, Pig!" cried Alec, with a groan of agony that came from the deeps of his soul.

"I *beg* your pardon?" said Dummer, who was sensitive about her weight but not strong-minded enough to eat less.

"Nothing," said Alec.

"*What* did you call me?" said Dummer.

"I didn't call you anything."

"It's the seal's name," said Kate. "Pig."

"Shut *up*," said Alec. For the second day running, he was furious with Kate. And now she had told Dummer Pig's name, which was none of her business.

"Ah," said Miss Dummer. Her smile had changed. Now she was showing a lot of white teeth; and she looked enormously *superior*. "What an *odd* name. Pig." She tittered. "*Not* the name one would have chosen for a creature of such poetry, such history." Alec's eyes began to glaze over. Out there in the loch, the rubber boats were still tied up alongside Ivan's trawler. That was the main thing.

"Well, I expect it is a very cuddly little thing."

"No, it isn't," said Alec.

"Don't be rude," said Miss Dummer. "I am sure it *is*."

"It could bite your hand off," said Alec. "Easy."

Miss Dummer looked at her thick wrist, then at Alec, who was glowering at her under knitted brows. "I'm sure you're wrong," she said. "Anyway, it won't get the chance. Now we know where it is, one of our – the Blue People's – boats will be going round to Solidaig to put the poor thing back in the sea, where its mother will no doubt find it. I shall tell them at dinner time."

"No!" said Alec. There was such desperation in his voice that Doris MacNab could not help sniggering. "He'll die!"

"Nonsense!" said Dummer. "The Blue People are scientists. They know what they are doing." There was a scream from the big schoolroom next door, and the wet crunch of a face hitting a wooden floor. Heavy Murdo at it again. "Well, I can't stand here all day. Next door, children. Alec, you will practise your scales. We will have another rehearsal this afternoon, third period. Now then. This morning we have a visitor."

She stumped next door and up to the dais at the end of the big room.

The school door opened and a head came

round. It had a scrubby beard, little round spectacles, a long, thin nose and protruding teeth.

"Ah!" said Miss Dummer, extending her arms in a sprightly manner. "Damien! Come in!"

Damien came in, dragging a sack behind him. Alec forgot that he was not on speaking terms with Kate, leaned over and said, "It's Oatcakes!"

"Now then," said Dummer. "This is Damien Stubbs, from the *Pole Star*. He's very kindly agreed to put on a show for us."

"About seals," said Oatcakes. He was very tall and lanky, with a clumsy look and a habit of sucking air through his prominent front teeth.

"I think Dummer's in love," said Doris MacNab, simpering. Heavy Murdo overheard and chuckled nastily.

"Now THEN," said Dummer. Tearing her eyes away from Oatcakes and picking up the chalk, she wrote on the board the word SEALS. "We all know the seal," she said. "The grey head bobbing sweetly in the water. But did you know that the seal is the most mysterious of British mammals?"

Nobody did, or if they did, they were not admitting it.

"Well, they are. When they come ashore to breed in the autumn, our scientists can study them closely. But when they leave to go to sea, nobody knows what happens to them. Yes, Murdo?" For Murdo was waving his hand in the air.

"We know fu' well what they do," said Murdo.

"And what is that?" said Dummer.

"They kill salmon," said Murdo.

"That has not been conclusively proven," said Dummer.

"What?" said Murdo, frowning.

"Nobody knows that is true."

"My dad does," said Murdo. "He's aye seeing them in the nets. And that's why he's away to shoot the brutes tomorrow."

"MURDO!" cried Miss Dummer.

Murdo looked smug. "It's my dad's living," he said.

Alec was miles away, wondering how he was going to get round to Solidaig at dinner time and stop the Blue People drowning Pig.

Dummer breathed deeply. She loathed Murdo, but even more she feared his father. Sometimes her imagination ran away on the subject of Ivan, and she saw him dressed in a kilt, sticking a spear right through some helpless Southerner.

"Well," she said. "I don't think he'll have much success this time. To explain why, here's Damien."

"That's right," said Oatcakes, stepping forward and sucking air through his teeth. "Hi, kids." He smiled. Alec knew that it was the kind of smile that meant someone was about to talk to him as if he was a baby. "We've come up here because we want everyone to be *aware* that it's no good shooting seals. Seals have just as much right to be on the planet as we have."

That sounded all right to Alec. He stopped himself drifting away and began to listen.

"So we were down in Oban yesterday and we heard from a friend, can't say who —" he winked, his eye horribly magnified behind his glasses — "that there was going to be seal shooting here. And we decided *no way*. So what we are going to do is go out in our Zodiacs, which are those kind of rubber boats, and get in between the guns and the seals. It may be legal to shoot seals, but shooting people is murder, right?"

The class nodded vigorously. Alec thought: this all sounds very brave. But if they feel so strongly about seals, why do they want to drown Pig?

"So to explain," said Oatcakes, "me and Flora Dummer will do some, like theatre." He rummaged in his sack while Miss Dummer rounded up a few tinies and made them struggle into Balaclava helmets.

Then he handed Miss Dummer a cardboard gun and she rushed around the dais crying,

"Pow! Pow!" The tinies in the Balaclavas lay on a rock made of pushed-together desks, pretending to be seals; while Oatcakes, waving a large blue flag with seagulls on it, rushed to and fro heroically getting in the way.

The Wester Aist Juniors sat there crippled with embarrassment.

Alec drifted. Then someone was nudging his arm with a sharp elbow and something was being shoved into his hand. A note.

He opened it. It said: *Sorry Alec I told my mum about Pig, Dummer got it out of her, forgive me. Kate.*

Alec read it twice, thinking about Kate's mum, who never left her alone. He was forced to admit that if old Babbler Robertson had started getting at him, he would probably have told her what she wanted to know. So he leaned forward until he could see Kate's freckled face and tight curls watching him anxiously. He gave her a slight wink. Her face went bright pink and a huge grin spread across it. Then he pulled a pen from his pocket, wrote on the palm of his hand: SEE YOU AFTER, and waved it at her.

"Two free periods this afternoon!" said Miss Dummer at last. "Within the hour, we shall be rescuing our first seal! I am declaring this Seal Day!" And she skipped off after Oatcakes like an airship following a vulture.

"What a dumbhead!" said Heavy Murdo, when the door was safely shut. "If he thinks he'll stop my dad, he's out of his tiny mind."

And for once in his life Alec was forced to agree with him.

He met Kate in the corner of the playground that was known not to be overlooked from the school windows.

"They locked up my boat," he said. "We're stuck."

"Oh," said Kate. She had gone white under the freckles. She started to say something, stopped, and started again. "We could use my dad's," she said.

Alec stared at her. "He'll kill you," he said.

Kate swallowed hard. "He won't find out," she said, as much to convince herself as Alec.

"He might," said Alec.

"Oh, come *on*!" said Kate. "Do you want to go to Solidaig or no'?" She paused. "What are you going to do at Solidaig?"

"Stop them," said Alec. "Let's go."

He had very little idea of how he could stop them. All he knew was that he had to get there fast. Heavy Murdo came past, a small child under his arm. The child was yowling piteously. "Leave him go, Murdo!" he said. "Pick on someone your own size."

Murdo flung the child away, flushed and angry. "I'll smash your face in one of these days," he said.

"You'd only dare do it from behind," said Alec. "So as long as I don't look over my shoulder, I'll be safe."

"I hope you said goodbye to your seal," said Murdo. "It's curtains for the lot of them, today."

"I thought you said tomorrow," said Kate.

"That was to put off old Dummer," said Murdo, with a blubbery leer. "They're beginning today. And you've helped, because Dummer and all them hippies is going off to Solidaig, to look for your seal.

"And when they've finished the other lot, they'll be back for yours. Yum, yum, woof, woof, lovely dog food," said Murdo.

Alec stared at him for a moment. Then he and Kate began to run for the beach.

Kate's dad's boat was long, made of wood. They pulled in the outhaul, climbed in and cast off. As Alec fired up the outboard, he knew that for the second day running he was committing the unforgivable sin: going through the Apostles was bad enough, but pinching someone's boat was ... well, it was so bad that he could never remember hearing about anyone who had done it before.

Still, there was no option.

On Ivan's boat, men were working. The Blue People's trawler was deserted. There was no pleasure in the buzz down the loch, round the Sound and along the coast inside the boom and wail of the Apostles. A school of porpoises rolled by, trailing green bubbles and grinning their cheery grins. Alec paid them no attention.

For as the white stripe of Solidaig opened out before them, he could see two black blotches pulled up on the beach. Zodiacs.

The Blue People had arrived.

Chapter Nine

As soon as the bow of the salmon boat hit the beach, Alec ran forward over the thwarts and leaped off. Kate followed. The Zodiacs were already some distance up the beach; the tide was ebbing. Fingers scrabbling, he bent the tripping-line on to the anchor, hung on to the end and shoved the salmon boat out to sea. When it was at the full stretch of the rope he jerked the anchor off the foredeck, and the boat swung to.

Kate was shouting at the top of the first hummock of sand. He ran up after her. *Please*, he said to himself. *Please let it be that Pig's hiding*. He came to the top of the bank.

Six Blue People were standing by the black blade of rock at the seaward end of the Sty. Alec had never seen that many people on Solidaig before. He did not like it. He began to run forward.

Kate kept up with him. "What are you going to do?" she said.

"Tell 'em about Ivan," said Alec.

They came over the rise and found themselves looking down into the Sty. The Blue People were now strung out in a ragged line across one end. Those in the middle were up to their waists in water.

"There!" said Alec.

A small green-grey arrow was streaking through the clear water towards the middle of the line.

"Look out!" said Kate.

The man in the middle of the line was Oatcakes. The arrow headed straight for him. He must have seen it, because he braced himself like a rugby scrum-half waiting for a pass.

"Swerve!" shouted Alec.

The arrowhead bore down on Oatcakes. But at the last moment, when it seemed certain that he would catch it in his hands, it swerved. The man made a despairing leap towards it and went flat on his face in the water. Pig shot through the line and into the part of the Sty where the water was deep and green and he could not be reached. There he floated on his back and gazed at his pursuers with innocent black eyes. The Blue People floundered towards him, except Oatcakes, who was shaking water out of a portable VHF receiver.

Alec stood for a moment and laughed. One of the Blue People went ashore and started pulling something out of a sack. A net.

"Make them stop!" yelled Kate.

Vaulting off the rock, Alec ran down to the knot of people. As he got close, he could see they were shivering. "Hey!" he shouted. "They're beginning! They're in their boats!"

The man untangling the net looked up. "What's that?" he said. He had a big red beard that fluttered in the chilly breeze.

"Ivan the Horrible. He's away after the seals."

The man with the red beard seemed to freeze. His eyes, Alec noticed, were like chips of blue glass: the eyes of a fanatic.

"They aren't starting till tomorrow," he said, still ladling net on to the sand.

"They said that to put you off!" said Alec.

"Nah!" said Oatcakes, who was standing dripping. "Listen, we're trying to rescue this seal."

"It's true, I tell you!" shouted Alec. "You stupid idiot!"

Oatcakes said, "Hey —"

The man with the beard interrupted. He

71

stared into Alec's eyes. Perhaps he saw in them some of the fanaticism that was in his own, because he said, "He's telling the truth."

He and the other Blue People ran back towards the sea, their wet clothes going flap, flap as they galloped. Alec stood and watched them. His school shoes were dry.

"What about Pig?" said Kate.

Alec looked at the head in the Sty and threw it a cockle. Pig caught it, tossed it in the air and caught it again. He seemed to want more entertainment.

"Sorry," said Alec.

They ran down to the beach. The Blue People were struggling with their inflatables, which had been left high and dry by the tide. Alec pulled in the salmon boat on its tripping-line, helped Kate in and stepped aboard without getting his feet wet. As he started the engine the Blue People were stumbling down the beach, lugging their inflatables and swearing.

They skirted the rocks in silence, keeping out of sight of the village. It was beginning to rain. Finally, Alec said, "Do you think that Blue lot will be able to keep up with Ivan?"

"I don't know," said Kate. "They seem a bit useless."

Alec nodded. He could still see Pig's head floating in the Sty, the innocence of the large, dark eyes. "What we need is to keep the Blue

People and Ivan bang next door to each other, so they'll get in each other's way and not bother about Pig."

Kate said, "We need a radio, really." They had about as much chance of getting at a radio as of dancing the waltz in the middle of the Sound. As far as she could see, there was no alternative but to get back to school for the last period.

She looked at Alec and opened her mouth to speak. It stayed open, but the words did not come.

Alec was sitting there as if in a dream, looking at something down the loch. She followed his eyes.

"A radio," he said, in a strange, tight voice.

"Yes," said Kate. "But where —" She stopped. Then she said, "Oh, *no*."

Because Alec was looking at the moorings. And the boat he was looking at was *Driller Killer*.

After that, things began to move very fast.

The salmon boat's bow shoved aside brown mats of bladder wrack in the rain-dimpled water under the rocks. On their port side, the little cove where Alec kept his boat opened out.

"Hang about here," he said. "I'm away to the house for a minute."

The path went up the hillside in a series of

73

zigzags. Alec did not use it. Instead, he went straight up the slope, keeping doubled up in the wet bracken. His breath began to rasp in his chest, but he kept low. If his mother saw him, she would shut him up indoors and that would be that. Alec thought guiltily that he probably deserved it, given what he was planning to do. Then he thought of Pig, and once again it became simple and straightforward.

The slope levelled out into the little plateau that held the house and the sheds. He paused, the sweat running down inside his shirt, trying to breathe as quietly as possible. The only sound from the yard was the rattle as the sow jammed her nose into her trough.

He stepped out and darted across the gap between the bracken and the nearest shed. Pressing himself against the rough granite, he inched across to the corner and looked round. He saw a slice of empty yard and began to edge along the wall towards it.

Buckets crashed in the feed store. Sweat squirted from his body and his heart hammered in his chest. His mother walked across the yard wearing a red scarf against the rain, her big shoulders pulled down by the weight of the bucket in each hand. She walked so close to Alec that he could almost have reached out and touched her. But she went past and the cow-shed door banged behind her.

Alec sprinted across the yard for the house door. He thought he knew where his father would be at this time of day. He was not mistaken.

From the kitchen came the sound of heavy snoring. Alec lifted the latch, very quietly, and put his head in. The range was burning fiercely and the room was full of a hot, stale smell with a petrolly overlay of whisky. In the armchair by the fire, Alec's father sat. His head was rolled against the chairback and his mouth hung open. There was a bottle and an empty glass on the enamel-topped kitchen table.

For a second, Alec looked at his father. He dimly remembered a time when he had not fallen into snores after lunch every day, when he had played his fiddle for fun, not just after he had been drinking whisky. In those days he had been good company. He had gone fishing then. He used to take Alec with him; that was when Alec had learned to use a boat. And he had painted the pictures that hung on the walls – heavy, exciting splodges of paint that did not look like people, but which gave you the idea of people all the same. But there was no time for thinking now. This was an emergency.

Alec tiptoed across the floor. The key to his boat's lock was on the nail above the sink, out of reach. He climbed up on to the draining board, grabbed the key, dropped it in his pocket. His foot caught something: there was a crash and splinters of glass shot across the red-tiled floor. Alec's father stirred. Alec ducked behind the table and went out of the door.

"Blasted cat," he heard his father's voice say, thick and gluey. Alec peered through the crack in the door. His mother was just going back into the feed shed. The key was warm in his hand as he shot across the yard, between the pigsty and the cow-shed, and plunged into the bracken. He slid down the hill and came to rest, soaked and panting, at the edge of the cove.

"That was quick," said Kate. Her face was pale and the muscles at the corners of her jaw stuck out as she tried to keep it from trembling. She was very scared, but determined not to show it.

"Yeah," said Alec, to whom it seemed the whole thing had taken about a day. He unlocked the mooring and pulled his boat in. "Listen. Take your dad's boat back and put it on the mooring."

"What about the rest of school?" said Kate, rather desperately. "We must be back for last period."

"You get back to school, if you're so keen," said Alec.

In her mind, Kate saw Dummer, glaring.

Then she saw the seal's head bobbing in the Sty. "No," she said, screwing herself up. "I'll come."

Over the wall of rock, the white bridge and upperworks of Ivan's fishing boat showed. "OK," said Alec, swallowing. "Let's go."

Chapter Ten

Alec was a master of moving about the loch unobserved; he had had a lot of practice, rowing in to school late. So while Kate moored her father's boat, he slunk up the shore, keeping behind rocks and moored boats, until she had moored and walked round the headland into cover. Then he went in to pick her up. As the boat grounded, he had a sudden thought. "Hop in," he said. Doubling up, he ran under the lip of the foreshore to the end of the school garden and up the line of the hedge. Dummer was back; he could hear the piano bashing with a fury unusual even for her, and the reedy tootlings of

Doris MacNab doing her best to sound like a whole recorder trio. He felt a sudden urge to laugh. But there was nothing to laugh at, really.

He went into the cloakroom and unhitched his satchel from the hook. Then he ran back to where Kate was waiting. "Food," he said.

Kate nodded. She sat tensely as he shoved off across the strip of smooth, dark water and sculled through the rain to the seaward side of the trawler.

Alec stood up. The side of Ivan's boat was a black wall. He saw it with horrible clarity, each little flake of paint, the trickles of rain, the brown rust-stains from the scuppers. He took a deep breath. Then he banged on the side with the butt of an oar. It rang like a gong. He shouted, "Anybody in?" and held what was left of the breath in his chest.

Gulls cried. Ripples clocked against the hull. Far to seaward, the Apostles muttered. There was no reply.

"Come on," he said. "Let's go." He heaved himself up the side, and tied the boat's painter to a stanchion. Then he hauled Kate after him.

They stood for a moment appalled by what they were doing. Rain fell, but the sky did not. Nobody shouted.

Alec said, "Keep down." The fishing boat had a high foc's'le. It was lying nose-on to the shore, so on deck they were invisible. They crept aft, to the pile of rusty white super-structure that held the bridge and the living quarters.

And the wireless cabin.

The steel door at the port side of the bridge opened easily. A smell of fish and diesel came out to meet them. "Come on," said Alec.

"What if there's someone here?" said Kate. But Alec had already gone. She took a deep breath to still her chattering teeth and followed.

Driller Killer was by no means a tidy ship. There were piles of rubbish everywhere and a heap of old beer cans tossed into a corner of the bridge. Alec opened a door. A smell of ancient socks leaped out at him like a dog. "Sleeping quarters," he said, when he had got his breath back. He tried the next door.

This time the smell was grease, hanging in brown stalactites from the ceiling and clotting the sides of an ancient chip pan on a slimy stove. "Third time lucky," said Alec, and shoved in.

It was the radio shack, all right. Someone had left the remains of a plate of sausage, egg and chips on the desk, and the floor was covered with torn-up weather forecast telexes. Alec cleared himself a space, and switched on the VHF.

A voice said, "OK, Jimmy, let's go to the

Jug!" It was warped by the static and a thick Western Highlands accent. But Alec recognized it immediately. Ivan the Horrible. The Jug was one of the rocky islands where the seals lay, out on the far side of the Sound.

"I'm with you," said another voice: Dense Dougal Tam it was, the radio operator of *Driller Killer*, in whose chair Alec was sitting.

"Away we go," said Ivan's voice. "Praise the Lord, and pass the ammunition."

"Why aren't those Blue idiots listening?" said Alec. He twisted the dial back to channel 16, the call channel. "Blue ship *Pole Star*, shore station," he said. "Blue ship *Pole Star*, shore station."

"Shore station, *Pole Star*," said a voice out of the speaker. It was loud because the *Pole Star* was only a few cables down the loch.

"Get down to channel 8," said Alec. "You can hear what the enemy are saying, then. And get a chart and the radar and look out for Ivan. He's a tricky swine. Over."

"Who's this?" said the voice on the other end.

"Pig," said Alec, and switched off the set. Then he said to Kate, "That should keep them hopping about. Let's have a peep."

They went through to the bridge. The rain had stopped. Beyond the big windows, sun glared up from the puddles on the hatch-covers. Alec found the On switch for the radar, dragged a stool over and climbed up to look into the rubber eyepieces.

"Let me see," said Kate. She had forgotten to be frightened.

"Hang on," said Alec.

The arm of the radar swept round its black background. When the beam brushed a rock or an island, it showed luminous green. Alec saw a sort of map of the Sound, the Twelve Apostles and to seaward, the Jug. Among the familiar outlines of the rocks were other, smaller echoes: things moving. There was a big blip over towards Eigg; a trawler, probably, going up to Ullapool. But what seized Alec's attention were the two tiny blips speeding towards the Jug from the direction of the Flatirons, another collection of rocks.

"Got 'em," said Alec. "Brilliant." He pulled away from the eyepieces. A couple of cables down the loch, *Pole Star*'s superstructure was spewing out people. Someone was running up her mast with a big, heavy pair of binoculars. He could hear the clank of her windlass as she pulled her anchor out of the sand, the chug of her diesels. The Blue People looked as if they had decided to take Ivan seriously.

"OK," said Alec. "They won't lose 'em now. Now we're going to jam Ivan."

"We're *what*?" said Kate.

Alec was grinning. He looked full of confidence. "Jam him," he said.

Kate shrugged. "Aye, aye," she said.

"Right!" shouted Dense Dougal Tam, looking up from his portable VHF and pulling the peak of the tartan bobble hat down over his eyes. "We're here!" His voice was hardly more than a hiss above the roar of the Zodiac's engine; but Ivan the Horrible, at the tiller, lip-read him and showed his dirty teeth in a grin. He throttled back.

"OK," he said. "So I'll get the gun out nice and slow and we'll like idle round to the other side of the Jug, and then we'll see. Take her, Jimmy."

Jimmy McColl took the tiller. The little rubber boat corkscrewed along just outside the heavy white water that surged back from the black rocks of the Jug. With the engine idling, the scream of the gulls on the rock was almost deafening. But Ivan hardly heard it. He pulled the rifle out of its canvas sock; an ancient Lee Enfield his dad had pinched in the Second World War, together with ten thousand rounds of ammunition and a small lorry. There was a lot of that in the Western Highlands, and very few policemen to ask questions.

Ivan wiped the oil from the barrel; old the rifle might be, but it was beautifully kept and deadly as it had ever been. He thumbed cartridges into the magazine and worked the bolt to put one up the spout. "OK, Jimmy," he said. "Let's go round. Slow, mind," he added at a roar as Jimmy pushed the boat half out of the water.

The black rocks flowed past. Ivan could feel the tube of the inflatable boat's side shove against his barrel chest under the dark blue jersey as the waves came under. "Get down!" he said.

The men in the Zodiac grovelled in the bilges.

A flat rock appeared in the blue slop of the sea. Its top was crowded with long grey shapes. Ivan's eyes searched the crowd until he found what he wanted. A big seal, with a little seal alongside. Mother and pup. Kill the pup, then the mother as she hovers by its side. Two for the price of one. "Eat my fish, would you?" he muttered. But it was hardly a matter of fish, any more. Ivan loved killing, and his blood was up.

He settled the foresight on the pup's neck, brought the backsight to cup it. Holding his breath, he waited for the Zodiac to rise on a wave. As it hung on a crest, he gently squeezed the trigger.

The rifle said *click*. It was a small sound among the roar of the sea and the cry of gulls. It was the last small sound Ivan heard for several minutes.

"Blasted old cartridges," he muttered, and

worked the bolt again. At that moment, he heard the snarl of an outboard engine the other side of the rock. The seals heard it too. They raised their heads, looked, listened, and slid into the sea. "Blazes!" hissed Ivan. And from the blind side of the island there shot a rubber dinghy flying the Blue People's flag, the wake streaming from her stern, the figures inside clinging on with one hand and waving triumphantly with the other.

Ivan raised his rifle. There was a seal's head in the water fifty yards away. His thick forefinger took up the first pressure on the trigger.

The sound of the Zodiac's outboard rose to a scream. Suddenly, he was not looking down his sights at the seal, but at a face with a bobble hat and round spectacles. For a split second, he was filled with a rage that nearly tightened his finger on the trigger. Then he thought better of it, put up his gun, and swore horribly in Gaelic. "How did they find us?" he said.

Dense Dougal shook his head.

"Call the other guys, ya tube," said Ivan. "Tell 'em the Toad. We'll lose 'em there." He pulled his whisky bottle from his bag, and grinned. The Toad was a tangle of reefs and ledges through which the tide ran like a salmon river. If they could get a hundred-yard start, the Blue People would never get near them.

Dougal said, "Don't work."

"Hurry, ye daft git," said Ivan.

"Something's weird," said Dougal frowning at the portable transceiver in his hand.

"Ach, give it here," said Ivan, reaching out a thick blue arm and switching it on. Then "Eek!" he said, and almost dropped it.

For out of the speaker came a dreadful, crackling singing. It was distorted, but even if it had not been it would not have been much fun to listen to. It was Alec and Kate, singing the Birdies' Song. And when one person is transmitting on a VHF channel, nobody else can use that channel until he stops.

When they had finished the Birdies' Song, Alec and Kate immediately began the dreadful Fingal's Cave overture. Ivan swigged whisky, and his face grew redder under the black stubble of his beard. Finally, he said, "It's bluidy kids. We're cooked. Off home." He snatched the tiller and throttled up so the engine screamed and the spray whizzed back from the transom. "And if I catch 'em," he said. "I'll tear the wee brutes limb from limb."

Dense Dougal looked at Ivan's hands. The fingers were like hard pork sausages, with letters tattooed across the knuckles. Dense Dougal's lips moved as he read what they spelt out. H—A—T—E.

Hat, thought Dougal, his large eyebrows meeting in concentration over his small pink eyes. Funny thing to get tattooed on you.

"*Wait* till I catch the wee swine," screamed Ivan, over the howl of the engine.

Chapter Eleven

"I've lost them," said Alec. "I think they've stopped transmitting. Let's get out of here." He ran to switch off the radio, and went out on deck. The snarl of outboards sounded from the point. They went down the side in a hurry and into Alec's boat. "Get down," said Alec. Kate crouched in the bottom. Alec began to row, hard, for the middle of the loch. He rowed so hard that he suddenly saw the school windows round the point. Quickly, he pulled into the lee of a lobster boat.

Too late.

Aist Primary was preparing itself for the day's end. Children were rushing to and fro,

looking for satchels and scarves and gum-
boots. Heavy Murdo was swaggering through
the crowd, waist-deep in infants, stealing
food.

Doris MacNab was gazing out of the window. She was deeply disappointed that Alec
had not turned up at the rehearsal. It was for
his benefit that she had gone home at dinner
time and changed into her new mauve dress
with the jitterbug petticoats.

Outside the window, a small dinghy with
a stub mast emerged from behind a lobster
boat. Alec was at the oars.

Doris's eyes narrowed to china-blue slits.
"Miss?" she said.

Dummer was trying to force a large boy
into a small anorak. "What is it?" she said,
crossly.

"Alec Whean's on the loch," said Doris.

Dummer sent the boy spinning. She clutched Doris's arm, and squinted out at the dazzle
of the sun on the water. "He is," she hissed
like a stout snake. "So he is." Abandoning her
charges to Mairi, the assistant teacher, she ran
for the bicycle shed.

Alec rowed quickly across the loch and into
the shelter of a headland. It had begun to rain
again, a fine drizzle that misted out the high
slopes of Beinn Dubh and softened the far
shore. Kate jumped over the side and on to a

rock. "What will you do now?" she said.

"Put the boat back," said Alec. "Return the key. Hope nobody noticed it was missing."

Kate contemplated the immediate future, and shuddered. "We're going to get into awfu' trouble," she said.

"Say we were at Solidaig," said Alec. "Blame it on me."

"But those Blue People saw us leave," said Kate.

"Huh," said Alec, with scorn. "They reckon we're just kids. As far as they're concerned, we don't exist."

Kate nodded. Then she turned and ran into the drizzle.

Alec went round to the boat cove, padlocked his boat, and set off up the hill for home. With a bit of luck he could get the key back on the nail before anyone realized it was gone.

Halfway up the path, he turned. The loch and the Sound lay spread below him, their edges softened by the rain. There were two Zodiacs on the beach: the ones from *Driller Killer*.

Ivan and his men would be in the Hawtrey Hotel by now, cursing. Three more Zodiacs were tied up at the side of *Pole Star*. That accounted for the lot of them. It looked as if Pig would be safe at least until tomorrow; and Alec strongly suspected that tomorrow, the Blue People would be too busy chasing Ivan round the ragged rocks to bother much about a lone seal pup. He started up the path in a cheerful mood. He wished he could tell his mother and father what he had done. They would not like it, though. Still, he felt pretty pleased with himself.

It did not last.

As he breasted the heathery rise behind the sheds, he heard voices. He stopped and fell flat on his face, his heart thumping hard. For he recognized the speakers.

One was his mother. The other was Miss Dummer. Both of them sounded angry, but they were too far away for him to be able to hear the words.

Cautiously, he crept across the wet grass until he was at the back of the cow-shed. He put his eye to a nail-hole in the corrugated iron. Dummer was standing in the yard. Her face was red, her pink cardigan beaded with the drizzle. "I saw him!" she was saying. "In his boat!"

"That's not possible," said Alec's mother. He could not see her, but he could hear from her voice that she was wondering. "Come into the house a minute."

"No, thank you very much," said Dummer in her insistent Home Counties voice.

"Well, then, hang on there a minute." His mother's voice had an edge of annoyance; she thought Miss Dummer was being a snob. He heard the door slam, and he turned and ran, back the way he had come, with the drizzle soft on his face. For he knew she had gone in to see if the key to the boat's padlock was on its nail.

He fumbled the lock open, climbed into the boat and booted it away from the shore. He got round the point by shoving with the oar. He knew that his ripples would scarcely have died away by the time his mother got down to check that the boat was gone.

He rowed carefully and quietly. The drizzle had come back and stolen the wind, and the water of the loch was like glass. Sound travelled very clearly across the water.

The first sound he heard was Dummer. "Ow!" she yelled, and there was a thump. The path was slippery with the rain.

"He's gone," said Alec's mother's voice. "He must have been gone for hours. How he got the key I'll never know. Was he by himself?"

"Ow," said Dummer, whining. "I've hurt my knee. Yes. He was alone in the boat. The *naughty* boy."

The rain thickened, lashing into the water with a heavy, sustained roar that drowned out the voices. Alec took advantage of the noise to put the shoulder of the mountain between himself and the women. Then he leaned on the oars, rocking on the oily swell running up the Sound from the open sea, thinking.

If he went home, he would never see Pig again; he was sure of that. The tides were getting bigger as the moon waxed. Say Pig's mother had been kept away from her pup by the thought of traversing nearly a mile of Solidaig beach in the open. She might come back at spring tides. So he had to give Pig a chance till then.

And he knew how.

There was an old bothy up in the dunes behind Solidaig. He would go there and keep watch; and if those Blue idiots came back, he would make sure they didn't catch a glimpse of Pig.

He was vague about exactly how he would do it; but the act of deciding cheered him, and he pulled along the shore with a new vigour.

The rain poured down. He was wet and he was hungry; he tried to ignore it. But the hunger pangs were severe. They made him wish he had his satchel.

His satchel.

His stomach stopped aching with hunger. Instead, it felt suddenly sick and seemed to roll over. He had taken the satchel aboard *Driller Killer*. He had not brought it off. It must still be there, on the floor of the radio cabin, with his name on the strap in black biro.

Chapter Twelve

Alec looked up at the sky. The cloud had come down, trailing dirty curtains of mist and rain across the sea. The shore was a dim black line fifty yards to starboard. Nobody was going to see him; he would have time to visit *Driller Killer*, retrieve his satchel and be at Solidaig before dark.

Pulling hard on his right oar, he spun the dinghy in its own length and started to row for the middle of the loch. As he went, he tried to concentrate his thoughts on Pig. That way, he did not have to think about what would happen if Ivan and his crew were out of the hotel already.

There was no wind at all. The clouds sank heavily on to the water and stayed there as mist. The *clonk* of his oars and the gurgle of water at his transom were the only sounds in the world. Then, so suddenly he almost shouted with the surprise, the black shape of the fishing boat loomed out of the fog.

There was no sound, no light. He drifted nearer on the tide, his heart making the sound of a huge drum. Then the sweating steel wall of the trawler was high above him, and he was fending off to stop the clang of wood on metal.

Alec tied up quickly, struggled up on to the hull, tied the painter to a ringbolt and went aft.

The bridge was blacked out. It looked as if nobody had been aboard since that afternoon. He slid inside. The mist threw the interior of the bridge into twilight. His satchel was on the floor under the radio desk. Bending, he grabbed it and slung it over his shoulder.

Fifty yards away, men's voices sounded, and someone started an outboard engine.

Alec was no coward, but he had done a lot of brave things that day and now he had the sensation that he had run out of courage. For perhaps half a minute he stood there in the smell of dirt, rigid as a rabbit in headlights, unable to move or think.

The outboard throttled up and grew louder.

Alec regained the power of movement. He scuttled for the bridge door, let himself out on to the deck, and ran, keeping below the line of the steel bulwarks, for the painter of his dinghy. His hands shook as he untied the round-turn-and-two-half-hitches. The outboard was getting closer. It must be Ivan.

The dinghy was directly below him now. He gave the painter a final pull. The movement slid the satchel off his shoulder, hooked the strap on the rail. It caught. The strap broke. Instinctively, he grabbed at it, caught it as it fell between the dinghy and the ship's side. But as he grabbed at it, the painter slid out of his hand. He heard the rattle as it fell into the bow of the dinghy. Then the tide caught the dinghy and it drifted quickly away into the fog.

No, said Alec in his mind. *This isn't happening.*

But it was.

On the other side of the hull, the outboard slowed. Open-mouthed with horror, Alec saw a thick-fingered hand reach up and grab the rail. The heads and bodies were out of sight. Across the knuckles of the hand were tattooed the letters HATE.

Frightened rabbits go into holes. Alec took one look round the rusty white deck. The cover was off one of the hatches. He had no idea what was down there, but there was not time to worry about that. Gritting his teeth, he dived in.

He could have landed on bare iron and broken a leg. Actually he landed on a pile of nets, rolled into a corner, and lay there stiff as a plank.

Boots rang on the deck and there was the sound of swearing.

Alec stopped breathing. The engine started: a heavy metallic chugging. Then there was noise forward, the whine of an electric motor and the clank of chain coming inboard. They were pulling up the anchor.

He forced himself to think, hard. If they were taking the boat out, they were going fishing. If they were going fishing, they would be using the nets. If they were using the nets, hiding among the nets was not very clever.

Cautiously, he tiptoed forward, under the foc'sle, until he came to the bulkhead that cut off the nose of the trawler like a steel wall. There was a hatch in the wall. The clanking of the chain was very loud up here, because beyond the bulkhead was the chain locker, where the anchor chain was stored after the windlass had hauled it aboard.

He opened the hatch and climbed in.

It was pitch dark in there. Chain crawled across his legs like a wet iron snake. It was very heavy. But *Driller Killer* had been anchored in shallow water, and it should stop soon.

It stopped. The boat's iron sides began to vibrate to the clatter of the ancient engine and a whiff of diesel fumes crawled forward. Alec settled down on his hard, slimy bed of chain to wait the night out.

After ten minutes, the bow started to rise and fall with a heavy plunging motion. He guessed they were heading out into the Sound. The day's rain had wetted his clothes and the salt water that came in with the chain had completed the job of soaking him. He began to shiver. The shivering took his mind off Ivan and the rest of them and settled it on himself. He was hungry, he realized. And the satchel, which until now had seemed like a pesky nuisance, suddenly became a huge bonus. In the pitch darkness he fumbled it open and found cheese sandwiches, oatcakes with honey and, best of all, in the thermos, hot chicken soup.

The soup warmed him up and he began to feel positively cheerful. But the food took the blood away from his extremities and the cold redoubled. He began to think of his mother, packing his lunch, and what she and his father would think when the dinghy turned up empty, on the rocks.

At the thought of the pain they would suffer, he felt the tears pricking at the back of his eyes. He gritted his teeth fiercely. Maybe he should go and tell Ivan to take him back, now. But then he would be kept in, for weeks maybe, and that would be the end of Pig. No. What he had to do was keep Pig in the clear until the spring tides. After Pig was free, he did not particularly mind what happened.

Some time later – in the pitch black of the chain locker, there was no way of knowing how long – the engine slowed. Feet came clanking into the hold and there was shouting as men heaved the nets up topsides. Alec waited, shuddering, listening to their ill-tempered yelling as they shot the nets. The cold was getting worse; he could no longer feel his fingers and toes, and he was getting sleepy, in a nasty, sickening way. He knew he could not afford to go to sleep, because when they came to drop the anchor and the chain started to fly inside the locker, he would be sleeping in a mincing machine.

He had to get out, before the cold got him. The voices outside continued. He felt himself slipping, weakening. All right, he found himself thinking, I'll count to a hundred. After that, I'll go out into the hold, whether they're still there or not.

He counted slowly at first and then, because he was so cold, faster. He could hardly wait to get out of this slimy little dungeon.

When he got to eighty-three, a voice outside said, "That's it!"

"Get up here then, ye lazy devil!" shouted another, on deck.

The boots banged. Alec stopped counting and struggled out of the hatch into the hold.

It seemed hot out there and almost dazzlingly bright. It took perhaps a minute for him to realize that the dazzling light was actually the moon, filtering down through the open hatch and that the warmth was only the sea air.

His head cleared. The moonlight left an oblong patch of silver on the weed-littered plates of the hold's deck. He slid past it into the band of deep shadow under the ship's sides. He was shivering so much he could hardly stand. Aft, he thought; there will be heat from the engine, aft.

Something soft and coarse caught his foot and he fell forward into the dark, biting back a yell of pain as he took the skin off his elbow. He pulled himself to his feet again. He had fallen over a pile of sacks.

They gave him an idea. It was to do with warmth. He grabbed a handful and dragged them behind him as he hobbled.

Along the aft end of the hold was a line of bins, designed to hold net-floats and leads. Alec pulled one of them open. It was half full of old newspapers and beer cans; the kind of thing you expected on *Driller Killer*. Still, it did not look as if anyone would be rummaging around it tonight. Alec climbed in and closed the lid after him. Then he struggled into a sack and huddled the rest around him.

It was better like that. The heat of the engine came through the bulkhead into the locker. There were scrabblings that might have been rats, but Alec was too tired to pay them any attention. Exhausted by the cold, wrapped in the disgusting smell of wet newspaper and stale beer, he fell asleep.

Chapter Thirteen

Alec was woken by the clang of feet. He had no idea how long he had been asleep; it felt like a long time, because he was stiff and cold and hungry, and his head felt fuzzy. He knew where he was straight away. First, he ate what was left in his satchel; it was not enough, but he had a feeling he would be needing his strength today. Then he shoved open the lid of his bin.

A pale, silvery stream of net was pouring down into the hold through the hatch. Alec frowned. The nets the fishermen used were normally made of green twine. This looked the wrong colour. There were three men in the hold. Two stacked the net in its pile, arranging leads one side, floats the other. The third man was receiving the yellow plastic fish-boxes as they came down the chute. What was in the boxes glittered in the grey light coming from the hatch: fish like bars of silver. Salmon.

Suddenly, Alec knew why the net was the wrong colour.

The boxes stopped coming. The engine's revolutions increased as the fishing boat moved to new grounds. The light in the hatch was growing; dawn was on its way. Alec began to feel hungry again. But he kept watching.

There were four men in the hold now, working at the pile of netting. There was a ragged hole in one end of it. They cursed. "Bluidy seal," they said, and cut the damaged part free, and made good what was left. Then they went on deck and started to shoot; letting the boat drift down the wind, paying the net over the side so it would hang in the water like a long curtain. Into this curtain would swim cod. And salmon. Alec sucked in his breath. His father had given up fishing, he had said, because there were so few salmon left that it was unfair to kill the survivors. But here was Ivan, massacring them. Not only massacring them, but blaming the seals for the damage he was doing himself.

The last of the net went up the hatch and overboard. Voices filtered down. They sounded thick and slurred. Alec knew from long experience with his father what made a voice sound like that: whisky. He crept out into the hold.

The boxes of salmon lay like chests of treasure against the forward bulkhead. Quickly he scooped up the length of net the men had cut off and stuffed it in the bin where he had been hiding.

Voices came from on deck. "That was a good night!" one of them said.

"Aye." It was Ivan the Horrible, thick and grating. "Except for yon seal that holed the net."

"Ach, well," said the first voice.

"Seals," said Ivan, and there was a silence thick with the sound of the diesels. "Let's go shoot some seals. Bit of fun, like. We'll get back before them hippies is out of bed, nae bother. But right now I'm away for a wee kip."

"Me, too," said the voice.

"She'll do on autopilot for an hour."

The other voice yawned. Boots tramped across the deck and the bridge door shut with a heavy clang.

Alec gave them five minutes. Then he went up the iron ladder from the hold and very slowly raised his head above the coaming.

Black fumes belched from the diesel stack. The sun hung like a red football over the jagged mountains to the eastward, spreading a blood-red carpet across the black sea. The lights in the bridge were on, illuminating its inside like an aquarium. Nobody stirred.

Very cautiously, Alec crawled out on to the deck. It was littered with salmon scales and starfish, and bits of crabs the men had smashed out of the net. He paused to take stock.

Driller Killer was marching along in the mouth of the Sound, heading northeast. A-stern, the great mass of Eigg reared from the sea. At this speed, they were a good two hours from the mouth of the loch and the nearest land was five miles away. No wonder Ivan had put the boat on autopilot.

Alec crept back into the hold and set himself to think. If he lay low and did nothing, he would get back safe and might be able to sneak off unseen while Ivan and his crew went shooting seals. But he had no more faith in the Blue People's ability to get up early than Ivan did. Which meant he had to stop them himself.

Bending low over the deck, he made his way aft, to the door of the bridge.

Chapter Fourteen

There was nobody inside. The wheel was moving in short, eerie jerks, driven by the autopilot. Turning the doorhandle with the caution of a dentist giving a filling to a hungry shark, Alec crept in.

The air smelt of whisky and cigarette smoke, the way the kitchen did at home after his father had been sitting up late. Alec walked quickly across to the autopilot. It was a simple compass dial, with an outer bezel bearing a red arrow-head. Wester Aist Primary was the kind of school where autopilots and similar bits of boat gear took the place of cars and footballs in the conversation. So Alec knew full well that all he had to do was twist the bezel to a new bearing and the boat would turn on to that bearing and stay there.

He twisted. The boat's nose began to swing, away from the distant cone of Beinn Dubh and on to the lower tump of the Wee Ben at the mouth of Loch Shiel, the next one south from Aist. He knew its outline well, because he had been there in his father's boat; and he knew the entrance, with the big Victorian fishing lodge behind it. At this distance the lodge was invisible, but he caught a flash of fire as the sun glanced from its windows.

He waited for the boat to come on to the course, his thumb hovering over the Lock button.

Beer cans clattered aft of the wheelhouse. The doorhandle rattled and there was the sound of cursing. Alec's thumb stabbed down on the button and his knees turned to water. He scudded towards the door and dived under the rickety navigation table just as Dense Dougal stumbled into the cabin.

All Alec could see were the man's feet and legs, clad in heavy ex-Army marching boots. The legs walked towards the wheel and Alec stopped breathing. But Dougal was not heading for the autopilot. Instead, he sat down in the helmsman's chair and put his feet up on the window ledge. Within two minutes, the tin ashtrays on the navigation table were vibrating to his heavy snores.

Alec slipped out of the bridge door and back into the hold. With Dougal on watch, *Driller Killer* was about as alert as a plate of mashed potatoes.

The thought of mashed potatoes made him hungry again. It was cold in the hold after the fug of the bridge. What was more, he had slept too little and he was tired. So he clambered over the mound of nets and into his bin, pulled the sacks around him, and went to sleep.

He dreamed. He dreamed that he was running across a high jagged ridge between two corries in the mountains and that there was a stag chasing him. Instead of antlers, the stag had hands that clenched and unclenched and on the knuckles were tattooed the letters HATE. Stones flew from under his trainers as he ran, booming down the cliffs of the corries. The stag was catching him. He could see the shadows of the hands from the corner of his eye, hear the roar of the breath in its great, bloody nostrils...

He woke up, sweating. The dream faded fast, but the roaring was still there and boots were hammering on the deck above his head, and there were voices, but the roar was too loud to hear what they were saying, except that they were blurred and angry. And frightened.

Alec came out of his bin at rocket speed. The deck was bucking like a bronco. He knew that roaring, and it scared him worse than Ivan the Horrible and all his men put together. It was the thud of water on rock, mixed with the roar of tide tearing through spaces so narrow that the water was twisted and tortured until it yelled for mercy. It was the voice of the Twelve Apostles, preaching. And when they were preaching this loud, below decks was no place to be.

He ran up the ladder and on to the deck. A wave knocked him flat and he grabbed an iron ring to stop himself slithering. The sun was shining out of a hard blue sky. Against the sky, tall pinnacles of black rock reeled and danced, stretching from one side of the world to the other. They were right in among the Apostles. Alec had no time to wonder how they had got there. One glance showed him what was happening. The engine was clattering at full throttle, fighting the tide and losing.

The water flowed in huge boils and swirls, kicked up by the fins of rock that stuck up from the bottom. The fishing boat lurched and swung as the man at the wheel fought the current. Alec hung on, feeling the spray of the halo wet on his face, watching the wall of the middle Apostle come up at him.

The helmsman saw it too. He slammed the boat into reverse. The engine howled. Blue smoke billowed from the exhaust and white propwash shot under the hull and swirled around the nose. But the tide was running at nine knots. Engine roaring, *Driller Killer* was borne remorselessly down on the wet black wall.

"Ahead!" roared Ivan the Horrible.

Gears clashed in the bowels of the boat. The tide grabbed her hull and flung her at the wall of rock. The helmsman's face was a white blur behind the windows as he spun the wheel frantically; too late. As the propeller bit, the side slewed towards the rock. Ivan shouted incoherently. There was a huge crash and a jar that knocked Alec off his feet.

"Power!" yelled Ivan. "Power!"

Lodged against the flat face of rock by the weight of water, *Driller Killer* shuddered as the helmsman fed power to her engines. Inch by inch, with a terrible scraping, she started to move along the wall.

"Go *on*," said Alec, to himself.

No one seemed to have noticed him. No one was doing anything except stare at that wall of rock as it inched by, and try not to think about what would happen if the boat spun and heeled and took water and went down, and they found themselves swimming in the cold green water rushing by the rocks with a sound like an express train.

"She's going!" shouted Ivan.

Inch by inch, she moved. The deck shuddered as if alive. "She's going!" he roared again, his heavy red face stretched into a grin that showed his black and yellow teeth.

Driller Killer moved forward. The tide got a wedge of water between her side and the rock, and hammered it in. Her stern came away. Her deck became a cliff as the tide whacked her in the belly and she heeled. The men roared, clinging to whatever they could find. Alec hung on to a ringbolt and shut his eyes.

There was another bang. The boat rocked, came on an even keel. Then the roaring was fading. But he still did not open his eyes. It was his fault that Ivan's boat had gone into the Apostles and if anyone had drowned, it would have been his fault too. No amount of saved seals could have made up for that.

"Well, well, well," said a voice like hobnails on broken glass. "Look who's here."

He opened his eyes and looked up at a circle of dark faces.

There was a very short silence that seemed to last a hundred years. Then Ivan said, "What might you be doing on my boat?"

Alec thought for a second. He was extremely frightened; but, he decided, he had to tell the truth. He took a deep breath and opened his mouth.

But Ivan forestalled him. "Somebody has

111

put my autopilot out," he said. "So I've lost a lot of paint and we're lucky we didn't sink." His big hand came out and grasped Alec by the jersey so the collar dug into his neck. He put his unshaven face close to Alec's. "Which is to say *you're* lucky we didn't sink. And what I am wondering," he said, "what I am wondering is this. Was it the same person who swamped out my radio yesterday has been fiddling with the controls today?"

Alec was not seeing the face. Instead he was seeing Pig, gazing at him with his large, calm eyes. "I don't know."

The big sausage fingers clenched in the front of his jersey. HATE, they spelt in the middle of the blue wool. He felt his feet lift from the deck. "Well, now," said Ivan, in a low, gravelly whisper. "He doesn't know. But I do." With his free hand he rummaged in the pocket of his grease-spotted blue overalls. "What's this?" he said. In his hand was a pencil. Down the side of the pencil in gold letters was printed ALEC WHEAN. "I found it on the radio cabin floor."

"My dad gave it to me last Christmas," said Alec. He knew it was the wrong thing to say, that he should be denying that he had ever seen it. But out here at sea, with the pumps going and Ivan's stinking breath washing over him, he was suddenly missing his father very badly.

112

"How did you get aboard?" said Ivan.

"In my boat."

"So where is it?"

"It drifted away."

Ivan looked at him through narrowed eyes, in silence. "So," he said. "Nobody knows you're here. I could just toss you overboard. I *ought* just to toss you overboard."

Alec felt very frightened.

"But I won't," said Ivan.

"Let me go," said Alec.

"No," said Ivan. "It's time someone told you where to get off."

"That's not your job," said Alec.

"Oh," said Ivan. "But maybe it is. Maybe your useless wee daddy needs a bit of help, if he won't do it himself. Useless boozer. Why shouldn't he do some work, instead of yon dam' fool painting? Any kid could do it better – OW!"

Alec had pulled back his foot and kicked him as hard as he could in the kneecap.

Ivan got control of himself. His face twisted in an ugly grin, and he said, "Siddown." He dropped Alec on the deck. He was not ready for it and banged his hip, hard. It hurt, but not as much as the foot Ivan placed on his neck.

"Listen, brat," said Ivan. "I told you before. We're working men, trying to feed our families. We net fish. Then seals take the fish.

We've seen 'em. So we're going to kill a few, and no wee dumb chums' league's going to stop us."

Alec tried to wriggle away, but the wet iron of the deck ground into his cheek and he could not move.

"Any road," said Ivan, "since you love seals, I'm going to show you what it's like to be one. I'm going to put you ashore on Lum Rock and you can talk to your pals. And maybe later I'll tell someone where I left ye."

Chapter Fifteen

They came down on the Lum from seaward, the engine thudding heavily. Alec sat on the deck, shivering, trying not to think what his dad was going to say.

The Lum was an eighty-foot cylinder of rock that rose from a jagged disc. Today, the dark blue sea was breaking white on its fringes.

"What a shot," said Dougal. "Ach, they're away."

The disc had been covered with the big grey shapes of resting seals. But hearing the engine, they slid into the water. A few heads watched *Driller Killer* as she laboured towards them.

They sank gracefully from view as the fishing boat came within range.

"Right," said Ivan, when they were thirty yards off. "Put the boat in the water."

Dougal went aft and released the dinghy from its davits.

"Get in," said Ivan.

Alec climbed in. Ivan came after him and took the oars. The chug of the engine receded as Ivan pulled for the shore. HATE, said the knuckles on the oars, coming and going as he rowed.

He came alongside the downwind shore, where a projection of rock made a natural quay. "Get out," he said.

Alec got out, feeling cold and hungry and frightened.

Ivan was glowering at him, watching him minutely. "Well?" he said. "Are ye scared?"

Watching him, Alec suddenly saw the resemblance between Heavy Murdo and his father. Murdo was a bully because he was thick; the only things he could spot, with his heavy, dull mind, were pain and fear. Now, Ivan was trying to produce that same effect. Alec did not intend to give him the satisfaction. He said, "I like islands."

Ivan's face became dark and threatening. Then he twisted it into his unpleasant grin, and said, "I hope you'll like them by the time you're finished with this one."

He tossed a plastic bottle of water on to the shore and pulled away. Alec walked round to the other side of the island, so he would not have to watch him go.

The dinghy went up in the davits. *Driller Killer* turned, water creaming at her stern, and passed fifteen feet away from the rocks. Ivan shouted, "I forgot yer dinner!" He pulled back his arm and threw something that bounced at Alec's feet. It was a big dogfish that had come out of the nets, still alive, writhing on the ground, darting looks of fury from its tiny, mad eyes. "Ye like seals so well, try their food!" roared Ivan. His noisy, stupid laugh sounded over the clatter of the engine. Then *Driller Killer* turned her stern to Alec and was gone.

The silence closed in, thick and solid. Alec booted the dogfish into the sea. Then he sat down on a rock and concentrated on not crying.

That lasted for about ten minutes.

He soon realized that there were more urgent things to do, like getting off the rock. Being taken home like a naughty boy, as and when Ivan decided to pick him up, would make him look a real idiot. The Lum was not a rock from which it was possible to paddle to the land without getting your knees wet. The mainland lay across a quarter of a mile of water. And it was not flat, swimming-pool water; it was blue, and it heaved, and now and then it broke into angry swirls as the tide flexed its muscles. Alec knew that only a suicidal maniac would go swimming there while the tide was running.

To seaward it was worse. The sea stretched seamless back to the Apostles and across to the islands three or four miles away, at the far side of the Sound.

Alec shoved his hands into his pockets and walked once round the rock, to warm himself up. There were bits of driftwood wedged in the boulders at the foot of the chimney, but nothing big enough to use as a boat. Gloom settled over him like a blanket – a cold blanket; he was hungry and his jersey was thin. But the wind was from the west and the sun was still in the east, so he scrambled up the base of the column of rock in the middle of the Lum. He found a ledge cushioned with tussocky grass and leaned back against the rock. It was as warm as he had hoped; he closed his eyes and watched the red shapes float on the inside of the lids, and soaked up some heat.

After perhaps ten minutes, he heard a movement below him. He opened his eyes.

Between his knees he could see a slot of rocky beach. On to that beach was heaving itself a seal. It dragged across the stones using its front flippers, looked around and evidently saw nothing that worried it. Then it heaved a mighty sigh, like a fat man who has climbed a steep staircase, and rolled over on to its back.

Suddenly, the sea off the rock was a-bob with grey heads and big black eyes. Singly at first and then in threes and fours, the seals heaved themselves ashore.

From his rock armchair, Alec could see five of them – two cows, who lay in the sun and snoozed; two young ones, a bit bigger than Pig, who must have been born late last autumn; and a bull, its back seamed with the white scars of old fights. The bull wanted to rest and the young seals wanted to play. While he rested his mighty bulk on the stones, the little seals made dashes at him, nipping him with their small, sharp teeth until he turned round and walloped at them with his fore-flipper, like a human father goaded past bearing. The young seals shot out of range and stayed quiet for a minute. The bull snarled, showing huge white teeth, as if threatening to eat them alive. One of the cows woke up and snarled at the bull; telling him to lay off her little Johnny, Alec guessed. The bull looked shamefaced and shuffled away. The cow went back to sleep, keeping one eye open as the small seals resumed their play.

Alec watched them for perhaps an hour. The sun marched round. His perch became cold and his muscles were stiff from staying in the same position. Reluctantly, he heaved himself up. The seals scuffled and plunged into the water. The thought of Pig set him wondering about escape again. He decided to climb the Lum.

It was an easy climb. The breeze was strong up here; it flapped his jersey against his arms and blew his hair straight back off his forehead. The tide had been going out for a couple of hours now and when he looked down he could see the dark fringe of weed round the Lum's beach. From this height, the sea was not a dark, uniform blue. Towards the shore, pale green sandbars lay just under the surface, merging with the white sand of Solidaig. He could see the flat mirror of the Sty. Rocks were dark shadows in the blue-green of the water. Where they had almost dried out, their brown fringes of weed turned the surface to glass.

Alec squatted among the fish bones and gull muck that crowned the Lum and gazed at the sea. There were no boats moving; there was only the cry of the gulls he had disturbed in his climb and the distant roar and thump of the sea in the outer rocks. Everything was as it had been for thousands of years.

He stiffened.

From the southern shore of the Lum, a line of dark shadow extended beneath the sea. It went on until he lost it in the distance, curving in towards the rocky point at the northern end of Solidaig beach.

He found a sheltered ledge and settled down to watch.

Chapter Sixteen

The tide ebbed. The sun rose in the sky; it became hot and his hunger grew. He drank from his water bottle and wiped the sweat out of his eyes with the back of his hand. The wind had dropped. The sea was like green satin, hugely inviting. The muscular swirls in the middle of the channel were few and far between: the tide had all but stopped running. And the black shadow under the water had dried out to become a dotted crescent of rocks, three quarters of a mile long, connecting the Lum with the point at the end of Solidaig.

Slack water is the time, thought Alec.

He took off his clothes, tied them into a bundle and fixed the bundle to his head with his belt. Then he climbed gingerly down to the beach.

The seals watched him from a hundred yards to seaward. He said, "Ow!" as he put his right foot into the water. It was like liquid ice. As he went further, it crept up his legs and over his stomach, so cold it seemed to burn him.

He walked forward over the stony bottom, gasping as the water covered his chest. Then the ground fell away suddenly and he was swimming towards the first of the crescent of rocks.

Alec was a good swimmer, if not a particularly stylish one. But he was nervous now. Though the sun was warm it was early in the year; northern Scotland is at almost the same latitude as Greenland, so despite the influence of the Gulf Stream, the water takes a long time to warm up. Alec swam as hard as he could, to keep the blood flowing; and in five minutes, he was slipping through the long, slimy weed on the fringes of the first rock.

He lost no time resting. He knew that he had to get to the Solidaig headland before the tide turned. So he plunged in again.

This time, the cold of the water was less of a shock. The distance between the two rocks was longer, but he was in his stride now and he covered it in the same time it had taken to get to the first one. When he looked back, the Lum seemed far away, with the black heads of the seals bobbing in the foreground. One more swim and he would be halfway. He felt suddenly lonely and exposed, crouching in the bladder wrack on this rock that the tide would cover twelve feet deep. As well as loneliness, he felt guilt. He was breaking the rules that kept you alive in a boat. He had taken a dinghy through the Apostles, interfered with Ivan's autopilot and now he had abandoned the Lum for the shore. In his mind, he heard his father's voice: *If you capsize, always stay with the boat. Try to swim ashore, and you'll drown.*

But it was too late for worrying now. Taking a deep breath, he plunged in.

It was a short swim, this one: about forty yards. But it was here that the trouble started.

He had taken perhaps fifteen strokes when he felt the bundle of clothes start to shift on the top of his head. Three strokes later, the bundle fell off. He made a grab for it and in grabbing he went under. The water was deep: his feet found no bottom. Until then, he had known that he was in the middle of the sea, swimming with nobody in sight; but it had been a matter of curiosity, as if it had all been happening to somebody else. Now, a foot below the surface, he realized it was happening to *him*.

He panicked. Panicking, he thrashed about. The belt came undone and his clothes scattered. Being wet, they started to sink. He thrashed more, felt his jeans slip beyond his reach, away into the blue depths. His jersey wrapped itself round his arm. Water got into his mouth. He choked, went under again, the salt bitter in his mouth. *This is no good,* he thought. *Much more of this, and I'll drown.*

The thought sobered him. As he came up, he gulped air. This time, it went into his lungs without added water. Still clutching his jersey, he swam back to the rock he had started from and hauled himself up into the sun.

Come on, he said to himself. *Get a grip, Alec Whean.* But it took him ten minutes to get a grip. And that ten minutes he spent shaking and shivering and feeling hungry and thirsty, and being quite, quite sure he was going to drown.

But he calmed down. At least he had his wool jersey, which would be warm even when it was wet. The rest of his clothes didn't matter. There was no fashion parade on Solidaig and nobody would mind if his bum was showing. Thinking of himself on the catwalk modelling a wet jersey and a worn set of Y-fronts, he began to giggle. And while he was still giggling, he tied the jersey round his waist by its arms, jumped into the sea, and swam to the next rock. It was as easy as that.

But when he came to the next rock, he saw something that sent the chills running down his back.

Before, the weed had floated straight up in the green, glassy water, moving only to the ripples of his splashy progress. Now, it was all beginning to lean to the southward, the fronds arranging themselves in parallel lines on the surface.

The tide had turned.

Chapter Seventeen

Alec did not give himself time to think. Instead, he jumped straight in and started swimming. He was aiming not at the rock itself but at the horizon to the left of it, so the tide would carry him down. It was a short swim, the first one. But it was hard work, because all the time he had to swim up-tide as well as across. And when he reached the rock and took stock, he was only just over halfway.

There was no time for resting now. The arc of rocks was curving in towards the headland and the tide, which had been partly behind him on the previous swim, was running directly across his course. When he landed on the next rock, he had to haul out and sit for a moment to catch his breath. Before his heartbeat had slowed, he was in again and swimming.

After that, the swim became a long nightmare of bitter salt, and slamming heart, and stomach aching with hunger. By the time he got to the second-from-last rock, the tide was really picking up and the tip was already submerged. He used it to kick off from and started for the last rock between him and the headland.

He knew he could not do it even before he started. It was a long swim – perhaps a hundred and fifty yards. The pull of the tide on him was like the current of a river. But there was no going back now; the rocks he had used for staging posts would be under water by the time he got back to them.

He struck out as hard as he could, heading to the left of the rock, as usual. But before he had gone thirty yards the tide had him and he was looking straight at his destination. And ten strokes later, he was looking not at black rock, but at empty sea. When he rose on the smooth blue swell, he saw, far away, impossibly far away, the long white sweep of Solidaig beach.

He swam back up for the rock. But the tide made a bow-wave under his face and the rock came no closer. His breath was rasping in his chest now and he felt cold and weak and very frightened. But most of all, he felt stupid. Stupid because what was happening to him was what happened to you if you fooled about with the sea. And when he had drowned, there would be nobody to look after Pig, over there, among the smooth humps and bumps of Solidaig...

He lay on his back in the icy water and let the tide sweep him down towards the Apostles. There seemed no point in doing anything else.

But as the rasp in his chest gave way to the creeping numbness of the cold, he knew that he could not just give up. So he started swimming again, not hard, but moving towards the shoreward edge of the tide, letting it push him, using it, not fighting it.

The land went by. The green mountains rising behind the beach looked tiny compared with the sea. The Apostles were a line of black cones; a seal's head came out of the sea between him and them. Alec wondered, vaguely – his mind was becoming vague, out here in the deep water – whether Pig would have helped him ashore, if he had been old enough.

The next wave came under him.

He saw the boat.

It was a dark blue salmon boat, two hundred yards away towards the shore. Someone was rowing it with short, canny strokes, stay-

ing in the lee of the rocks at the south end of
Solidaig, out of the tide. Alec knew the boat,
knew who was rowing it.

It was his father.

He shouted.

It was a bad shout, weak and hoarsened
with salt. It would not carry. He waited for
the top of the next wave and stabbed his hand
into the air, moving it from side to side. But
he needed his hand to stay afloat. He sank
and, being tired, took a long time to come up
again.

When he had blinked the water out of his
eyes, the boat had moved up-tide. It looked
further away.

"Dad," he shouted again.

It was thin and weak and it died on the sea
without an echo. Tears filled his eyes. *Look
round, Dad*, he thought; *look round*.

But the figure in the boat kept its head
turned towards the shore, as if looking for
something or someone.

"Da —" began Alec.

There was a swirl in the water ten feet
away and a seal's head came up. The big
liquid eyes gazed on Alec with mild surprise,
the stiff whiskers trembling faintly in the new
breeze. Then the seal sank smoothly away.

Alec was too tired to shout. He watched the
blue boat, his eyes blurred with hopelessness.

Between him and the boat, there was a

commotion in the water, a mighty splashing that he could hear even with his water-filled ears. Alec saw the water and in the middle of it a grey body, rolling and thrashing and splashing. It's ill, he thought; it's been shot, it's caught in a net...

But the thrashing stopped and the seal's head floated fifty yards way, serene and even a little smug. And the figure in the boat was looking; Alec could see the face white under the old tweed hat. Lifting his leaden arms, he waved.

The figure in the boat stood up. Alec waved again, went under, swallowing water. When he came up, the boat was end-on, rowing towards him. The seal had gone.

Things got very hazy then. Afterwards, he thought he remembered the seal's head close to him in the water, watching him with a curiosity that seemed mixed with anxiety. He got the feeling it wanted him to swim. So he swam, although his arms and legs tried to drag him down. As the boat came up, he had a vague memory of the seal opening its mouth, showing its great fangs in a fierce white grin and then sinking away. He thought he saw it, but afterwards he could never be sure.

Then he was being lifted into the boat, smelt tobacco and whisky and felt himself being rubbed dry with something: a shirt, perhaps. He lay in the bottom of the boat with a jersey over his shoulders. The oars started again. There was another noise mixed up in them. His father was crying.

It made him feel extremely depressed, as much as he could feel anything. But then his father patted him on the shoulder, as if to make sure he was actually real. And that made him feel better and, feeling better, he let himself slide into a comfortable black bowl of sleep.

Chapter Eighteen

Alec woke up with a jump. He was in his own room, in his own bed, under the sloping ceiling. The bedclothes were smooth, as if he had not stirred in the night. There was a grey, rainy light filtering in at the window in the gable. He knew instantly that it was after midday.

His first thoughts were of Pig. Nobody had fed him for two days. He must be starving.

He ran down the steep stairs. His legs were a bit stiff, otherwise he felt fine. When he came into the kitchen, he stopped. There were other things besides Pig to worry about. His mother and father were waiting, grim-faced on the far side of the table.

"Maybe you'd like to explain," said his mother. She looked pale and there were extra lines on her face. She was tired; tired because she had spent a day and a night thinking that Alec was drowned. Alec began to feel very sorry indeed.

"All right," he said. He told them everything that had happened since he had gone aboard *Driller Killer* to use the radio. The only thing he left out was Kate Robertson. He did not want to get Kate into trouble.

When he had finished, there was a heavy, echoing silence. His mother was gazing at him with eyes that had dark shadows slung underneath them. His father lit a cigarette, looking at the floor.

The silence went on and on. He felt washed out, emptied by his confession.

Finally his mother said, "Go on." She was talking to his father. "Say something."

"Aye." Usually, his father looked nervous and worried. Now, he looked almost happy. "I fed your seal. Kate Robertson took me over to it at Solidaig."

"Great," said Alec. "Was he all right?"

"Sure."

Relief flooded him.

"Ach," said his mother, a snort of disgust. "The child goes away a full day and a night, his boat washes up. And all you can talk about is feeding seals."

"I'm not going to wallop him," said his father. "He'll not do that again in a hurry. Will you, Alec?"

"I will not," said Alec.

Suddenly his mother stood up and stumped round the table and hugged him, hard. Then she walked out into the yard and the buckets began to rattle.

"Come away," said his father. "I'll walk you to Ecky. Your boat's a wreck. Your mother let you sleep this morning. But you look all right now, so you can get off to school."

They walked out of the house together. It was a fine, blue afternoon with a smell of wet bracken. The hill was full of the noises of the morning's rain creeping towards the sea. Alec felt he must be dreaming. Perhaps he had drowned. His mother never hugged him. And his father always did as he was told. Something had changed and he did not know what it was. Whatever it was, he liked it fine.

As they walked down the path to the slipway, his father began to talk. "Ivan," he said. "I don't like Ivan at all." Alec had never heard him speak so frankly. His voice was quiet, as if he were talking to himself. "He shouldn't have put you on the Lum Rock. It was a bad thing to do. A wicked thing. He's a devil and that's all there is to it." He stopped walking and turned to face Alec. "Do you know what he once did to me? Us?"

"No." Alec felt that something odd and solemn was about to happen.

"I used to have a fishing licence," said his father. "To catch salmon running up the loch to the river. Ivan thought I'd be catching fish that he might have caught. The bailiff was a friend of his. So he got my licence taken away." He shrugged and smiled, his nervous, self-effacing smile, and walked on.

"Why didn't you get it back? Why didn't you fight him?" Alec could feel the anger like a balloon in his chest.

"If you fight someone like that, you come down to his level," said his father. "Anyway the fishing was losing money." He laughed. It was a clear, honest laugh; the laugh of a man who had got something off his chest.

Alec knew what was different today. His father was talking to him not as a child, but as a grown-up.

They were coming down the last of the path now, to the granite slipway. Ecky was there, mumbling a fag, his little blue eyes glittering. "Helloo, helloo," he said. "It's Robinson Crusoe II. Ye got away, I hear."

Alec was thinking hard and only nodded. He was very proud to be treated as a grown-up by his father. But he could not agree with him about Ivan.

*　　　　　*　　　　　*

He walked quickly along the far side of the loch. As he approached the school, a figure came out to meet him. It was wide and it waddled. It was Heavy Murdo, wearing a Celtic T-shirt and a malicious grin. He advanced like a blubbery tank. "Wa-hey!" he said. Alec presumed it was supposed to mean something.

"What's your problem, dwarf brain?" said Alec.

"I heard my daddy found you on his boat," said Murdo. "I heard he got you and he set you on the Lum."

"So?" said Alec, walking quickly to get away.

Murdo grabbed his arm with hard, grinding fingers. "He's no' finished yet," he said. "Nobody messes with my daddy. He's away to kill any seal he can find and he's gone to Solidaig special to kill yours first. And he said for me to be sure you didn't make any more trouble."

Alec stared in horror at his smug, beefy face. "Liar," he said.

"Hah," said Murdo, scornfully. "Get away into the school."

Alec tore his arm free. Murdo's thick lip was curled. He was telling the truth. "I'm away," he said.

"No," said Murdo. His fist came round and collided with the side of Alec's head. Alec staggered back.

Murdo came in again. He walloped Alec in the stomach and on the nose. Alec fell down. Murdo started to kick him. Alec saw a foot coming, caught it, got up, keeping Murdo hopping on one leg. Then he lifted the leg and heaved him back into the dustbin shed. There was a terrible crash. Murdo staggered to his feet, picking ashes out of his coarse black hair. "I'll tell my dad!" he whined.

There was silence in the playground. A little kid looked at Alec, eyes wide with joy.

Into the silence there came a tiny noise.

The air was still under the grey cloud that cut Beinn Dubh off at its shoulders. It carried sound well. And the sound it carried from away to the north was a light popping, like fat in a frying pan.

But it was not fat. It was rifle fire, and it came from away towards Solidaig.

Chapter Nineteen

Alec stood stock still for perhaps twenty seconds.

Then he began to run. He ran not for the loch and the boats that were moored there. He ran for the school and through the three little girls playing in the empty classroom and kicked open the office door with a bang that roared in the open spaces under the rafters.

Miss Dummer looked up, her egg-shaped spectacles giving her eyes their usual look of sheep-like surprise. As she recognized him, the lines of her mouth hardened. She opened her mouth to speak. But before she could get a word out, Alec said, "Come on!"

She inflated herself like a toad. "I don't —"

"They're shooting the seals!" shouted Alec.

She said, "Oh, that's all taken care of. We had a tip-off. The Blue People went to Moidart."

"The Blue People went the wrong way! Ivan's away to Solidaig!"

"Solidaig!" said Miss Dummer, and stood there with her mouth ajar.

"Quick!" shouted Alec.

"*Really!*" said Miss Dummer, sounding like a punctured air cushion.

"Come *on!*" cried Alec. He grabbed her by the wrist, and yanked her out of her chair. She weighed about twelve stone, but she was so amazed at one of her pupils laying hands on her that she came.

"What are you *doing?*" she cried. She was being dragged across the room now, her lace-up brogues slithering on the parquet floor.

"I need your help," said Alec. "*Please!*"

Though he didn't know it, those were the words that saved him. Flora Dummer was a lonely woman who was dying to be part of Wester Aist. And because Alec was clever and knew the place like the back of his hand, she had the idea that if she could get him on her side, she would have the place cracked.

So instead of jerking her hand out of his and giving him the lecture about truancy she had planned, she let herself be dragged across the playground. And when Alec stopped to say something to Kate Robertson, she stood like a lamb until he had finished. Only at the playground gates did she remember to turn and shout, "Read at your desks till I get back!" Then she started to pound after Alec, who was pelting down to the slipway by the loch. As she ran, she felt a tremendous joy.

Alec was talking to Ecky. "I need your boat," he said. "For a few hours, just. You get away to the hotel."

Ecky's eyes were shifty and doubtful. "Your dad said to bring you to school," he said. "Not to lend you the boat."

"It's an emergency," said Alec. "Plus, if you lend us the boat, Miss Dummer will buy you a bottle of whisky."

Ecky's bright blue eyes shifted towards the teacher, who was breathing hard, her face purple. She looked dazed for a second, then nodded.

"I'll take ye," said Ecky, looking nervously round to make sure Alec's father was safely over the other side of the hill. "Get in."

Miss Dummer stepped. The boat rocked. Ecky slammed it into gear and they chugged off up the loch.

"This *is* exciting!" cried Miss Dummer, and wrung her plump hands in ecstasy. Her face was shining, and she glowed with the satisfaction of at last being *part of things*.

Out in the swell of the Sound, she began to feel less confident. The heave of the waves was very big and the wind cut through her pink cardigan. Part of things or not, she was being led by an eleven-year-old child across a rough sea towards men with guns. She began to miss the support of the Blue People.

The boat hugged the coast, passing inside the Apostles. But their roar chilled her even more than the wind. When she glanced round, Alec's square jaw was set, his snub nose jutting towards Solidaig like the ram of an old-fashioned battle cruiser. He was not wearing a jersey, but he gave no sign of cold.

Ten minutes later Solidaig stretched out its white arms and gathered them into its bay.

"OK," he said to Ecky. "In here'll be fine."

Ecky shrugged. The bow grounded against the hard sand. "Let's go," said Alec.

"Twenty minutes," said Ecky. "Then that's that."

"We'll be longer," said Alec. There was no sign of Ivan or his men. But someone was firing a rifle in the rocks to seaward of the Lum.

"I can't wait," said Ecky. "I've got tae swim the bull across the loch to Mrs Morpurgo."

"Ach, well, thanks for the lift," said Alec, whose eyes were already searching the white sand up towards the Sty. "You might as well

142

go, then. We'll walk."

"Walk?" said Miss Dummer. But Alec had already jumped out and was running up the slope of the first sand-hummock.

"It's OK," said Ecky. "It's only ten miles."

"Ten *miles*?" said Miss Dummer, climbing over the side and landing with a splash that sent chilly water up her kilt. She did not remember ever having walked ten miles in her life.

"And a wee bit swim across the loch," said Ecky. "Still, you could be lucky and get a ride. Bye for now!"

She watched with a sort of fixed horror as the boat chugged up towards the dark blue horizon. Then she turned and began to stumble after the prints Alec's feet had made in the hard sand.

Alec ran, his feet thumping the hummocks. As he ran, he made mental notes. There were no tracks on the sand. That meant nobody had been here this tide – since midnight, say. But he had been out of action all yesterday. True, he had watched Solidaig from the Lum and nobody had come. But he had not been watching all day...

He came over the last hummock and ran down the far side, to the black blade of rock that closed the Sty off from the sea. There were bits of weed draped at its base, left by the high tide. The tides were growing with the moon; soon, maybe today, the water would be sluicing into the Sty and Pig would be free.

Pig.

He ran round the end of the blade. The Sty was a placid sheet of grey, reflecting the sky like a metal mirror.

"Pig," he shouted. "PIG!"

Nothing happened. His stomach froze with despair.

"PIG!" he shouted again.

From out beyond the Lum, rifle fire boomed.

The heavy clouds drifted by. Birds called. There was no Pig.

Something panted behind him. He half turned. It was Dummer. The sight of her filled him with anger. He had made her come because he had had an idea she would help; Ivan would listen to her. But now she was here, she just looked big and squashy and useless.

"He's gone," he said, his voice strangled by the lump in his throat. "Your rotten friends have taken him away."

Miss Dummer looked surprised and unsure of herself. "No," she said. "No, I don't think so." She stood for a moment staring into the still, deep water. Her chest inflated like a paper bag about to pop.

She began to sing.

It was a weird noise. It sounded like a cat

144

wailing at the bottom of a septic tank. Alec stared at her with his mouth open.

Eventually, she stopped, one hand flung out, head tilted, eyes closed. "Seal Joy," she said, complacently. "The old Gaelic song of the shore. It will call your seal, if anything will."

Alec watched the Sty, too embarrassed to say anything at all. Dummer was completely round the bend.

The water rippled. A head came up, bang in the middle, and made a snort of disgust that summed up exactly how Alec felt.

"Pig!" cried Alec.

Chapter Twenty

Alec leaped into the air and came down grinning and waving his arms. Pig grinned back and drifted nearer, sending a gentle bow-wave from his chin. Then he saw Miss Dummer and stopped.

"It's all right," said Alec. "That was her, singing." He was actually somewhat awed at her success. But there was not much time for awe. "You poor old bloke, you must be starving," he said. Bending, he began to rake cockles out of the sand, twist them open and throw them to Pig.

"*Well!*" said Miss Dummer. "That was ever such a good spell." For a moment she saw herself as a witch, stout and powerful, charming Wester Aist.

"Would you mind giving him a few cockles?" said Alec. She picked up two cockles and twisted them open. "Ugh," she said, as innards slid between her soft fingers.

"Pig likes them," said Alec. And indeed, Pig was whizzing round in tight circles, playing tag with the cockles and pretending to be surprised every time he won. Alec watched him with delight.

But even Pig could not make him forget that Ivan was out there in the islands and if he had told Murdo he would work round to Solidaig, that was what he would do. And even if Ivan did not come, the spring tides were here now; the sea was licking with long tongues up the dips in the beach. Little by little, the tongues were licking away the dry land. There was an hour and a half to go before high water. At this rate, the Sty would be flooded out long before then and Pig would be on his own in the open sea. Alec realized that the idea of things magically changing had been wishful thinking. Pig was the only seal in sight. He would not be swimming out to join the others on the spring tide; he would be alone in the great grey waters of Solidaig. He thought of himself, yesterday, swimming, struggling against the tide. It would be like that for Pig. No seals would come to help him; Ivan would make sure of that.

He stood up. Dummer was grovelling for cockles, her large kilt stirring in the breeze.

"Sing again!" he said.

"Oh!" said Miss Dummer, coyly. "I'm not sure it would *work* again. It is very strong magic, and a little exhausting —"

"Sing!" shouted Alec.

"What for?"

"They're shooting them out in the islands. We'll call the seals in here. They can look after Pig. Then we'll put ourselves between them and the guns."

"B...between them?" Miss Dummer's mind suddenly filled with a picture of Ivan the Horrible, large as life, squinting down the sights of a weapon the size of an elephant gun.

"Come *on*," said Alec. He tossed Pig a final cockle, waved, grabbed Dummer's arm and sprinted down the beach.

Dummer blundered into a water-filled trough, fell over and stumbled to her feet again. The beach was flooding rapidly.

"Now," said Alec, when they were standing up to their knees in cold water. "Sing, now!"

Dummer was wet and discouraged and the thought of Ivan's gun had stopped her believing in magic.

"But it doesn't *work*," she said, tearfully.

"Last time was just a *fluke*."

"That's not what you've been telling us at school," said Alec. "You told us that people and seals understand each other. You said one of your ancestors was a seal."

"Well..." said Miss Dummer. Actually, no Dummer had ever been a seal and she had been trying to make herself more interesting by pretending that one had. "Not a seal *as such*..."

"It's our only chance," said Alec. Miss Dummer had never seen a child so determined. *He believes me*, she thought, between pride and despair. *He believes me.*

"Oh, very well," she said. She inflated herself and began her weird crooning.

Out in the rocks the sea heaved. Gulls shrieked above the distant roar of the Apostles. Nothing happened.

"Louder!" said Alec.

She tried again. The seas stayed empty.

When Alec looked at her next, he could see that she was beginning to cry. He found that he suddenly felt sorry for her.

He touched her on the arm. "Maybe they can't hear," he said. She shook her head. Her face looked red and somehow young.

He rummaged in his pocket, found the two pieces of his bagpipe chanter. "Again," he said.

"But it won't *work*," sobbed Dummer,

tears pouring down her face.

"Try," said Alec.

They tried. Alec did not know the tune, but he managed something close. Dummer's caterwauling and the thin, eerie wail of the chanter floated out over the sea, which had fallen flat as glass.

The final notes died away; an echo came back off the faces of the rocks to seaward.

Miss Dummer said, "It's no —"

"Look," said Alec.

Out among the rocks, a black dot appeared on the surface of the sea. It might have been a pot-buoy, but there had been no pot-buoy there a minute previously. It was joined by others and others still.

"Again," said Alec. This time his voice was a whisper.

Miss Dummer began to sing and Alec to play. Slowly, the crowd of heads – there must have been eighty or ninety of them – came closer.

They played the tune twice. Miss Dummer's voice grew stronger as her confidence grew. Alec began to walk backwards, very slowly, drawing the seals on into the bay.

By the time they were in the shallow water, Alec's lips were stiff and sore. He kept playing, his eyes on the open water. Suddenly he stopped, in the middle of a verse.

Round the back of the Lum came two black

inflatables. In the sudden silence their engines snarled like angry hornets. Their noses settled over the white furrows of their wakes and aimed for the bay.

"Here they come," said Alec.

"What will we *do*?" wailed Miss Dummer.

"Get between the seals and the bullets," said Alec. "Are you ready?"

"Yes," said Miss Dummer, before the part of her that wanted to say no had a chance to speak.

The inflatables were very close now. Alec could see that Ivan was in one of them, with a couple of other men. In the other, Dense Dougal was waving a rifle as if he planned to storm Solidaig and claim it for the Scottish Cretins party. Alec did not give himself time to think. He ran along the water-covered sandbar. Between him and the boats the seals' heads slid under the surface. He looked down where the shallow water over the sandbar shaded away into the dark turquoise of a deep channel. Down in the blue-green, a fleet of great silver shadows shot by, heading for the land.

When he looked up again, the black rubber boats were slopping in the waves just off the beach. They were so close he could see the pimples in Ivan's black stubble. Ivan said, "It's that blasted kid!"

Alec was jumping up and down, as if on

151

springs. His blood felt as if it were bubbling like a kettle; he could not stop himself.

"Get oot a my way!" said Ivan, with an evil snarl. "Otherwise ye could get shot when I shoot them beasts."

"No chance!" cried Alec. "No chance at all!"

"You little devil!" roared Ivan. "Get clear!"

"No way!" yelled Alec. In an ecstasy of defiance, he stuck his thumbs in his ears and waggled his fingers. Terror and elation wrestled within him. "Yaaah!" screeched a voice on his left. It was Miss Dummer. She was standing calf-deep in water, crouching forward at Dense Dougal's boat. She also had her thumbs in her ears and her fingers waggling.

"Arright!" roared Ivan. "You have been warned!"

Inshore, seals' heads broke surface. Ivan raised his rifle, pointing it past Alec. Alec found himself running, leaping to get in front of the little black muzzle of the gun. Ivan swore, jerked the gun the other way and aimed quickly. The sound of the gun rattled in the northern corries of Beinn Hourn and a plume of water went up twenty feet beyond the right-hand seal.

"Missed!" roared Alec, beside himself with triumph.

"Kindly cease shooting at my pupil!" cried

Miss Dummer, who was bulky enough to be completely blocking Dense Dougal's view.

But Dougal was not looking at Dummer. He was staring southward and his mouth was hanging open. "Oh ma Goad!" he said. "Will ye look at that?"

He jerked his thumb down the Sound, towards the point where Beinn Dubh heaved its huge shoulders out of the water.

The clouds were lifting and dividing. A rift had appeared in the overcast and through it the sun poured down in golden rays, as if from the projection box of a huge cinema. It lit up the blue sea and green land and the ice-white of water, breaking. And it lit up three inflatables, trailing long feathers of spume. From the transoms of the inflatables flapped great blue banners with a device of waves and seagulls.

"Hooraaah!" cried Miss Dummer in a high, strained voice.

The Blue People were coming.

Chapter Twenty-One

Here they come, here they come, here they come, thought Alec. But he had very little time for thinking, because at that moment there was a great roaring of engines and Ivan's rubber boat reared its nose in the air, swerved, and came pounding through a gap in the sandbar. Five seconds later, Dense Dougal followed. Ivan's boat zigged and zagged furiously in the maze as he stirred the tiller like a man making porridge. Alec's stomach went cold within him. *I should have known*, he thought; *Ivan knows the beach as well as I do.* He began to run along the sandbar and on to the next, heading back for the fin of rock that cut off the Sty from the sea.

Another shot rattled among the black cliffs of Beinn Hourn. But Ivan had squeezed it off standing in a bucking boat and it missed by a mile. The seals were right in among the gullies now, hard to hit among the hummocks of white sand. But all Ivan had to do was go ashore and leave his boats to block the gullies and the seals would be bottled up, sitting targets...

To seaward, the outboards of the Blue People were a swarm of mosquitoes. Trailing arrowheads of foam, they droned round the headland and set their noses at the beach. Alec was standing on dry land now and Dummer had caught up with him. She was jumping up and down, waving her arms.

Alec started to wave, too. Then he stopped. His hands hung limply by his sides and his mouth opened to shout. But nothing came out; he knew what was going to happen, and it was too late for shouting.

The Blue People came on in line abreast, howling down on the smooth water at the edge of the beach. Whoever was steering did not know Solidaig, had no idea of the sand ridges that ran out under the deceiving glass of the sea.

They came at the beach at twenty-five knots, engines wailing like chainsaws. There was a shattering crash as their propellors slammed into the hard sand. Then their three shear pins broke at once and the engines screamed on up, meeting no resistance, and died, leaving silence.

After the silence, the Blue People started to shout at each other.

Alec opened his mouth to shout, too. Then he realized he was going to need all his breath and began to run back up the beach towards the Sty.

Ivan and Dougal were moving slowly now, wading out of their boats, digging in the anchors, getting ready for a long, leisurely slaughter. Alec shouted, "Stop that!" Ivan's head turned, and he distinctly saw the black and yellow of the man's teeth as he laughed at him. Then he turned away.

Alec went mad.

He looked down for stones to throw. There were no stones in the firm white sand. So he made a beeline for Ivan, splashing through the creeks, swimming when it was too deep to wade. As he came over the last bank he saw that in front of Ivan the sea had made a big lagoon, spreading along the base of the Sty's blade of rock as the tide came in. In the lagoon there glided, huge and silvery, the pod of seals that had come ashore earlier. As he watched, a wave of tide swept along the blade of rock and a gully of water gurgled round the end connecting the lagoon to the Sty. And down the gully, flapping and flopping with a pleased grin on his smooth grey baby's face, came Pig.

Ivan's gun went up. Alec covered the last five steps in mid-air and hit him slap between the shoulders. There was a huge explosion next to his ear as the gun went off. He started to hammer at Ivan's head with his fists. It was like hammering a brick, but he kept at it, keeping his eyes shut, so he did not have to see Pig's corpse thrashing by the edge of the water.

He felt himself grabbed, flung, flying through the air. His shoulder hit the sand with a terrible bang and he rolled in the water. Someone was cursing. "Missed, by God!" he roared. It was Ivan's voice. "I'll get him when he comes up!"

Alec shook his head. His shoulder hurt. Then he began to crawl. He did not crawl back up the beach, though.

He crawled into the lagoon.

People were shouting. The water became too deep to crawl. He began to swim.

The water was cool for his shoulder. Soon, he was in the middle. He turned, treading water.

He was looking down the barrel of Ivan's gun.

Then he looked beyond the gun, to the face. And on the face he saw fear and uncertainty.

"Come back!" shouted a voice. It was Miss Dummer. She was holding Dense Dougal round the body, so he could not raise his arms to aim his gun. "Come back!"

Alec hurt, a lot. The hurt reminded him of how tired he was. Tired enough to sink. But he kept treading water with feet like lumps of lead.

A face came up: large eyes, long whiskers, little earholes. Pig. "Pig!" cried Alec, joyfully. Suddenly he felt a great peace. He was very happy to be next to Pig in the water. He was very glad that Pig was not dead. He was so happy he knew he was going to cry.

He tried to stop himself. "It's all right," he said to Pig. "I'll stay." Pig looked pleased. But Alec knew that if he stayed, he sank. And if he went, Pig was dead, and so were the rest of them. There were heads all around him now, packed close, with their great moustaches of whiskers, their warm, faintly fishy breath...

He began to sink.

As he sank, he thought he heard a huge voice roar: "IVAN McPHEE AND DOUGAL TAM, LAY DOWN YOUR ARMS. YOU ARE UNDER ARREST."

Then the water closed over his head.

Chapter Twenty-Two

The next thing Alec knew, apart from choking and the burn of salt in his throat, was a pair of arms going round him. He could feel wet wool against his face. It was not the hard wool the fishermen made their jerseys from; it was soft and the arms underneath it were soft, too. He felt himself being dragged out of the water. Then he had to concentrate on coughing and spluttering for a while. When he could think about anything but breathing, he opened his eyes.

Miss Dummer was standing over him. She was soaking wet, her pink wool jersey and kilt sticking to the billows of her body.

"Are you all right?" she said. Something had changed about her voice, thought Alec hazily. It had lost the hooting soupiness that it had had before. Now it was an ordinary person's voice. He preferred it.

"Yes," said Alec.

"You're a twit," said Miss Dummer. But she grinned as she said it.

Alec got up, remembering what had happened. His throat was still raw and his head ached. The sun was out. It lit the sand a dazzling white, so he had to screw up his eyes. Out in Solidaig bay, a low grey Fisheries Protection vessel was cruising. The Sty and the lagoon were joined now, the blade of rock an island. The seals' heads were above the water. Pig was whizzing round and round one that had the white patch of an old scar, as if overjoyed.

Inland, five figures were stumbling up the first rank of the dunes: Ivan and Dougal and his crew.

Out at sea, the Fisheries boat sounded its siren. On its foredeck was a small figure, waving something in the air. Kate Robertson. Alec waved back, both his hands over his head, his hurts forgotten.

"What's that she's waving?" said Miss Dummer.

"A bit of a net," said Alec. "What happened?"

160

"Oh," said Miss Dummer, "that Fisheries ship turned up out of the blue. They shouted at Ivan and he ran for it. Jolly lucky, I call it. Is that Kate Robertson on the deck there?"

"It wasn't lucky," said Alec. "We arranged it. Kate brought the boat."

"She *what*?" said Miss Dummer, forgetting her English. "What are you talking about?"

"There are two kinds of gill net you use to catch salmon," said Alec. "There's legal net, made out of twine, sort of string stuff. And there's illegal net, made out of nylon monofilament, which is like transparent fishing line. It's deadly stuff, because salmon can't see it in the water. Well, when I was on Ivan's boat I thought the nets he was using were the wrong colour. So I had a closer look, and I saw they were monofilament. That's how he was catching all those salmon. So I scavenged a bit and stuffed it in the bin where I was hiding, and Kate went aboard *Driller Killer* and pinched it out of the bin and took it to the Fisheries inspector. Now he's come to ask Ivan how it came to be there."

"Goodness!" said Miss Dummer.

"Brilliant," said a new voice. It was one of the Blue People: Oatcakes, the man with the little round glasses. "They'll fine him five thousand pounds, confiscate his boat. It's what they deserve, swine like that."

Alec looked past him, up the beach. Kate

was coming towards him, walking beside a thickset man in a blue jersey. She looked extremely proud.

"This is Mr Andrews," she said. "From the Fisheries Protection."

"I want you to arrest that man," said Oatcakes, pointing a bony finger at Ivan, who was scrabbling up the face of a white dune inland. "On charges of using illegal nets —"

"Aye," said Andrews, who had a set, hard face with eyes that glittered as if he were keeping serious only with difficulty. "That's why I'm here."

Alec stared at Oatcakes. His face was pale and pinched, and his teeth stuck out like a rabbit's. He looks mean, thought Alec. Mean and vengeful, like Murdo in a mood. He took a deep breath. "Er..." he said. "Have you got any ... proof?"

"Proof?" said Oatcakes. "Of course. A length of monofilament net."

"Who found it?" said Alec.

Oatcakes said, "Listen, kid, I really don't think this has much to do with you."

"That's not what Kate Robertson said," said Andrews mildly.

"Go on, Damien," said Miss Dummer. "Let him answer."

Oatcakes frowned and directed a hurt look at her.

"I know who found it," said Alec. "Kate

162

Robertson did. In the bin, aft end of the hold on Ivan's boat."

Kate nodded. Alec winked at her.

"Hmm," said Andrews, his humorous eyes glittering above his heavy cheeks. "How do you know?"

"Because I put it there."

In the silence that followed, Alec stood rocking with exhaustion. He could hear his father's voice: *Don't come down to their level.* If he turned Ivan in, that would be the end of him; *Driller Killer* would be seized, the McPhees would go bankrupt, leave for Glasgow...

"Why?" said Andrews.

Alec looked him right between the eyes. "I just did," he said.

Andrews had seen a lot of life, up and down the west coast of Scotland. "So there's no case," he said. "We can't prove anything."

"That's right," said Alec.

Oatcakes tried to butt in. "Shut up, Damien," said Miss Dummer impatiently.

"Because if he has any illegal nets, he'll burn them," said Alec. "And maybe you could be keeping a bit of an eye on him anyway."

"We will be," said Andrews grimly. "Never fear."

"This is *outrageous*," squeaked Oatcakes. "How *can* you —"

"Shut up, Damien," said Miss Dummer. "This is a local problem. You haven't the first idea how these people live. Nor have I, for that matter."

"Sounds like you could be learning," said Andrews.

Alec was not listening. He was looking out over the great blue sheet of Solidaig Bay, where the water lay smooth as glass over the maze of sandbars. In the middle of the sheet were two heads: two seals, one large, the other small. The small one was Pig. The bigger one had a white patch on its head: the one Pig had raced round in the lagoon.

The tide had turned. Slowly the pair of them swam out into the deeper blue of the Sound, away from the mountains to where the Apostles hazed the sky and beyond, towards the far line of the western horizon.

EVACUEE

Gabriel Alington

Young Fanny Clegg is evacuated to America to escape the wartime blitz of London – while her brother Hugh joins the Royal Navy. Sent to stay with her "Aunt" Bird, Fanny finds herself in an unsettling world of sophistication and luxury. Bird's daughter Pepper seems friendly enough, but her son Jay is openly hostile. And, as Fanny soon discovers, he is not the only one.

"Many girls will identify ardently with Fanny in her trials."
Geoffrey Trease, TES

SOMETHING RARE AND SPECIAL

Judy Allen

Following her parents' divorce, Lyn has to move out of London with her mother to a temporary home on the coast. At first, missing her old friends and city life, Lyn feels like a fish out of water in this bleak, empty landscape, but then she discovers Bill Walker and his binoculars – and something very special...

This is a beautifully written and atmospheric story by the winner of the 1988 Whitbread Children's Book Award.

"A sensitive story, rich with thoughtful atmosphere."
Junior Education

THE FIRE OF THE KINGS

Julian Atterton

To young Osric and his cousin Edwin, heirs to the kingdom of Northumbria, Aethelfrith, the Grey Wolf, is the greatest hero in all of 7th century Britain. But, as they soon discover, the difference between friends and enemies is often just the length of a sword – and no man is ever safe from treachery...

"Julian Atterton is one of those writers who possess the gift (not very common) of being able to think himself convincingly into the skins of opposing people and causes – he has done extremely well."
Rosemary Sutcliff, TES

ANANCY-SPIDERMAN

James Berry

Anancy, the hero of these twenty lively and intriguing Afro-Caribbean folk tales, is both man and spider. Seemingly defenceless, he is an artful rogue who uses his cunning to outwit his opponents – the mighty Bro Tiger in particular. But these are just two in a colourful cast of characters which includes Bro Dog, Bro Monkey, Old Higue Dry-Skull, Swing-Swing Janey and many, many more.

"James Berry retells these vivid stories...in a soft, mellifluous voice that captures the magic and trickery of the spider hero."
Julia Eccleshare, Children's Books of the Year

THE SWORD AND THE DREAM TRILOGY

Janice Elliott

The King Awakes (book one)
The Empty Throne (book two)

Outcast from the City with his mother and baby sister young Red finds a Britain devastated by a nuclear holocaust and inhabited by savage tribes: Outmen, cannibals, Magickers and War Lords. Pursued by the evil Guardians, Red's one hope of survival lies with a mysterious stranger – a soldier called Arthur, woken from the distant past to fulfil a famous legend...

"A most inventive fantasy of a future world."
The Times Literary Supplement

"An exciting tale of quest and pursuit."
The Listener

A FEW FAIR DAYS

Jane Gardam

Enter the weird and wonderful world of Lucy's childhood. Meet Aunt Fanny, Auntie Bea and Aunt Kitty (who never stopped travelling). Discover for yourself Jinnie Love's Fair Days, nanny-nuns, akkerbeests, polycarps and queeds. Marvel over the stories of Mr Crossley's wig, the great ship, the magus Zoroaster and the beast in the mire...But, above all, prepare to be thoroughly entertained!

"Jane Gardam writes beautifully both for children and adults...An enchanting book."
The Lady

"A modern classic...It's a very evocative book."
BBC Radio

VAMPIRE MASTER

Virginia Ironside

There's something very sinister about Burlap Hall's new biology master, Mr. A. Culard. He hates light, loves bats and eats dead flies! Now the other teachers are starting to behave oddly too. The question is: will young Tom and his friends, Susan and Miles, manage to get their teeth into the problem before it gets its teeth into them?

"A very funny novel which keeps up a steady pace of entertainment and suspense."
The Bookseller

"Entertaining...Hilarious moments."
Junior Bookshelf

THE HORN OF MORTAL DANGER

Lawrence Leonard

When Jen and her brother Widgie stumble across a secret underground world, they find themselves in the middle of a war between two rival factions, the Railwaymen and Canal Folk. It is the start of a thrilling and dangerous adventure.

"A fantasy whose words are forcefully visual, whose concept is original and compelling."
Growing Point

"A lively, original and exciting adventure story."
The Times Literary Supplement

THE WATER CAT

Theresa Tomlinson

It's 1953, coronation year. Jane and Tom have just moved with their parents from Sheffield to the steel-working village of Carlingrove. Unimpressed at first, they soon find themselves involved in an intriguing 400-year-old mystery. The mystery of the "water cat"...

"Superbly blends fact and fiction...Theresa Tomlinson's stunning first novel for children ebbs and flows like the sea."
TES

"Unpretentious, compelling magic."
The Sunday Times

THE ARPINO ASSIGNMENT

Geoffrey Trease

It's 1943. One moment young Private Rick Weston is peeling spuds, and the next he's parachuting into occupied Italy on a vital and dangerous assignment, organized by the top secret Special Operations Executive. His mission? To find and assist the Resistance in their fight against the Nazis...

"Stirring, romantic and highly entertaining... A splendid piece of story-telling."
Leon Garfield, TES

THE QUEEN OF THE PHARISEES' CHILDREN

Barbara Willard

Whitbread Children's Book of the Year 1984

Moll and Sim Swayne and their children, Willow, Delphi, Fairlight and baby Star, have no home – they travel from place to place, taking shelter where they can. To young Will, Moll is a fairy creature, Queen of the Pharisees. But not even her special magic can save the family from the harsh fate they suffer, following Delphi's discovery of a gold guinea in the forest one day...

"A powerful historical story. A challenging but rewarding read."
Books for Keeps